Welco
The Accidental Mystery Series.

Books in the series:

And So To Sleep
And So To Dream
The Wrath of Grapes
And So To Love
And So It Goes
The Wrath Of Winter

BookLocker.com, Inc.
2013

First Edition

THE WRATH
OF
WINTER

EVELYN ALLEN HARPER

TO LOGAN,
MY NEWEST GRANDCHILD

CHAPTER 1

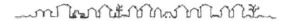

IN THE WHITE WORLD of snow that was falling like heavy wet cement from a blackened sky, the bolt of lightning followed by a crash of thunder seemed eerily out of place. Except for the police van that plowed through the deep snow, the road was empty.

The solitary man in the back of the van was viewing the whole situation as an adventure. Even though his shackled feet were attached to the van's security bars and his hands were cuffed, he intended to make the most of every minute. This was the first time he, Sammy the Grunt, had been out of his cell since his transfer from an overcrowded federal downstate prison to a much smaller northern one. Huddled under the warmth of the borrowed coat that covered his orange prison suit, he relaxed; the storm was the guards' problem, not his.

Hidden by the pelting snow, the wildly swinging traffic light seemed to appear out of nowhere.

"It's red!" yelled the guard in the passenger seat.

"Can't help it!" exclaimed the white-knuckled driver. "I can't stop!"

The unexpected carnival-like ride sensation as the van slid sideways and fishtailed through the intersection made Sammy grin; the front passengers didn't.

"I don't like the looks of this," muttered the driver. "Man, I'd love to see a snowplow right now!"

"Seems like we've been driving forever," the passenger whined. "Are we there yet?"

"Are we there yet, Daddy?" the driver mocked in a child-like voice. "You sound just like my four-year old!"

"Well, are we?"

"Almost. The dentist office should be straight ahead, on your right."

Another bolt of lightning followed by crashing thunder startled them.

"Wow!" cried the guard. "Lightning and thunder in the middle of a snowstorm? Who ever heard of that?"

"Thundersnow."

The guard whirled his head around and stared at the prisoner. "What did you say?"

"It's called thundersnow."

"How do you know that?"

Sammy shrugged. With years behind bars and lots of time to read, he had learned a little bit about many things. What he remembered about thundersnow was that a very powerful winter storm usually followed.

He kept this information to himself as they continued driving into the storm.

CHAPTER 2

THE VINEYARD WORKER shivered and pulled the flaps on his hat down over his ears. The accumulation of snow he'd found on the vines in Sarah and Albert's vineyard didn't worry Clarence; snow would protect them from the freezing temperature. What did worry him was the force of the wind, the depth of the snow, and the distance between where he was now, and where he wanted to be. Never before had the long walk from the vineyard to the house seemed so daunting, and never before had he walked through such wet and dense snow. Each step was a struggle.

Along with the pelting snow, the storm had brought early darkness. Unable to recognize landmarks, nothing looked familiar; for all he knew, he could be walking in circles. He didn't realize how anxious he'd become until he'd climbed a slight rise in the land and saw, in the distance, a light from the house; he hadn't lost his way home.

Warmth and safety were within reach; all he had to do was walk toward the light. Letting out the breath he'd been holding, he grinned to himself. He could almost feel the heat from the fireplace that awaited him. Just one step at a time toward the light…he could do it.

He stopped walking to watch a streak of lightning as it raced across the sky. Wow! Whoever heard of thunder and lightning in the middle of a snowstorm? Ready to resume his homeward trip, his eyes scanned the darkness, looking for the lighted house.

What had happened to the light? The fleeting relief he'd felt when he'd seen the lighted house was now replaced by a sinking feeling in the pit of his stomach. Without a light to follow, how was he going to get home? Had he shifted positions when he raised his head to watch the lightning's trail across the sky? If he hadn't, then all he had to do was walk in a straight line. Putting his head down against the howling wind, he blindly pushed on, one step at a time, through the dense and deepening snow.

CHAPTER 3

SAMMY THE GRUNT had been looking forward to being out of prison, but the darkness of the day and the snow piling up on the windows had turned the van into nothing more than a moving cell. Sammy rubbed his tongue over the stumps of his teeth and winced. At least the air inside the van was warm; breathing cold air caused him excruciating pain.

On the day that Sammy's toothache had reached the screaming point, and the other inmates were clamoring for him to shut up, the prison dentist had been rushed to the hospital with a burst appendix.

His aching teeth had become unbearable. When Sammy the Grunt pleaded with the guards to do something to put him out of his misery, an appointment had been made with a local dentist. The unexpected snowstorm had not been part of the deal.

Another lightning strike lit up the sky, followed by a booming clap of thunder. Wow!" exclaimed the driver. "That had to be clos…"

The top of a lightning-struck pine tree smashed through the windshield, cutting off the driver's remark. His foot slipped off the accelerator, his head smashed onto the steering wheel, and the car, drifting its way into the ditch, stalled. The guard in the passenger seat, impaled by a sharp branch in his neck, was spraying blood.

Sammy, unhurt in the back seat, sat in shock. He watched as the blood from the passenger's injury spurted with every heartbeat…until it stopped. The driver, covered by branches, wasn't moving. Never once had Sammy entertained the idea that a trip to the dentist could turn into a chance to escape. How could he not take advantage of this unexpected and unplanned gift? The newness of the situation momentarily stunned him until the chill of an unheated car brought him back to reality. But then, how could he do anything, chained as he was in the back seat?

In the front seat, buried under bloody branches, were two unmoving guards; one of them had to have a key. The passenger had bled out, and the driver wasn't moving. Sammy figured that if he was going to do anything, it had better be quick.

The front seat was in two sections with a console between the driver and the passenger. Stretching his long arms, he was able to reach the driver. What was the chance that the only pocket he had access to in his shackled position would be the one pocket with the key?

Straining with everything he had against the restraints, his shackled hands plunged into the pocket. Wonder of wonders, his fingers curled around a key. Slowly, his closed hands emerged from the pocket with a key safely within a fist.

Unlocking the shackles on his feet and freeing himself from the van's security bars was easy; freeing his hands was another matter. While cursing and frantically searching on the floor for the key that kept slipping through his fingers, the cuff finally dropped from his one hand. Freeing the other hand was easy.

With the increased rage and howl of the snowstorm filling the van, Sammy realized his freedom was still in question. Even though the guards weren't moving, the intensity of the storm was growing. He was ready for the next step, but was a next step even possible? Walking through the snow against the wind wasn't such a good idea. He knew he wouldn't get very far on foot, and he had no desire to freeze to death. The road was still drivable for those whose vehicles had four-wheel drive. He'd heard the guards talking about how glad they were that the van was equipped with it.

With mounting excitement, Sammy rubbed his wrists to get the circulation going. Wild thoughts were racing through his head; without even asking for it, freedom had been handed to him. He needed to disappear, but how? Peering out the window at the deepening snow, he realized his prison-issued slippers wouldn't get him very far.

In the front seat, buried under the top of a pine tree, were boots. He needed to remove the boots from one of the guards, and it had to be done fast. He searched for the door handle.

There was no handle. The police van's back doors couldn't be opened from the inside.

CHAPTER 4

SARAH SOOTHED THE crying baby as she stood in front of the picture window, staring out at the accumulating snow. Clarence was out there, somewhere. He should have finished his vine inspection and returned to the house by now.

"No sign of him?" asked Albert as he joined Sarah at the window.

"No sign of anything! Visibility is zero out there. Albert, what if Clarence is in trouble?"

"Clarence can take care of himself, but in case he does need help, I've turned on lights in the house. He should be able to see them from the vineyard."

The house seemed to shudder as a lightning strike knocked out the power. The only sound in the dark house was the wailing of three-month old Paul.

"What now?" Sarah asked

"Can you get Paul to be quiet? I can't think!"

Sarah rocked the baby in her arms. "Shhhhh," she whispered. Baby Paul shrieked louder.

Albert covered his ears. "I thought babies slept a lot. How'd we get one that does nothing but cry?"

Sarah didn't even bother to acknowledge Albert's question. "Albert, there's a flashlight in the kitchen cupboard over the stove. The other day when I was looking for something, I ran across a kerosene lamp. It's somewhere in the house, but I don't remember where. Clarence is out there in this storm, maybe lost. If we can find the lamp and put it in the window, he'll have a better chance of making it home."

"Man, it's dark in here. Ouch!" Albert muttered as he knocked his shin into something sharp on his way to the kitchen. "The furnace is off, so it's going to get cold in here pretty quick. Good thing I chopped firewood last week because the fireplace is going to be our only source of heat."

Sarah's comforting sounds and Baby Paul's cries followed Albert into the dark kitchen.

"Found it!" he yelled to Sarah. Expecting to see a beam of light when he turned it on, he choked back a curse when nothing happened. The batteries were dead.

"Sarah, where do we keep the candles?"

"Look in the junk drawer. I'm pretty sure there's one there."

A crash and a yell were followed by words a baby shouldn't hear. In a protective move, Sarah pushed Baby Paul's ear against her breast and placed a hand over his other one.

"Hey, I found it."

"Just one?"

"Yeah, and it's just a little one."

"That's what I thought. Albert?"

"Yes?"

"Remember when you went to the store yesterday, I reminded you that we were out of matches?"

"Oh, shit!"

"Albert, the baby! Did you find the flashlight?"

"Uh, yes, I did find it, but the batteries are dead. That's why I was looking for candles."

Silence.

"Albert, were you ever a boy scout?"

"We could be in serious trouble, and you're asking me if I was ever a scout?"

"Yes, I am. Aren't scouts taught to make a fire by rubbing two sticks together? Because that's what you're going to have to do if we want light from the candle and heat from the fireplace."

"Oh, shit," Albert grumbled.

CHAPTER 5

SAMMY LOOKED WILDLY around. Two dead guards, pieces of smashed windshield glass, and the top of a tree occupied the front seat. How badly did he want to escape? Badly enough to force his body over the back of the front seat to land on top of a dead man lying under bloody branches? Was there even room for his body in that crowded space?

One look at the bloody guard in the passenger's seat, and Sammy knew that wasn't the route he would take. The driver looked dead but he wasn't bloody, so when Sammy heaved his body over the top of the seat, he aimed for the driver's side despite the steering wheel.

Pine branches cushioned his landing on the wheel. Sammy paused in his escape long enough to cackle, "Saved by a goddamned Christmas tree!"

Opening the door and literally falling out of the van, Sammy ended up in deep snow. He needed boots, but to get at the driver's feet, he had to pull him out of the van; the branch made that impossible.

Did he want to escape badly enough to pull the branch back out through the windshield? Sammy didn't hesitate. Jumping up on the hood of the van, he threw his whole body into the task. Inch by inch he dragged the branch back out, working up a sweat. He took a brief rest on the hood, breathing hard.

Once the driver's seatbelt was unfastened, one pull and the body slid out of the van and into the snow. Sammy removed the guard's boots, opened up the back door, crawled back into the van, and easily exchanged his slippers for warm winter boots. Wiggling his toes, he was pleased to find that they fit.

A walk around the van to the passenger's side took effort. Sammy couldn't remember when he had walked in such dense snow. Unfastening the blood-spattered seatbelt was a messy job, but it had to be done. Once it was opened, it was easy to pull the guard out into the snow.

Now what? He was free, he had a car, two guns, and two pairs of handcuffs, but he was still wearing the prison-issued orange jump suit. Both guards were tall, but the driver was the taller of the two, and his uniform was free of blood. How hard would it be to remove clothes from a dead man?

He was about to find out.

Not wanting to leave his orange suit behind, he kept it on and pulled the driver's uniform over it. When dressed, he brushed pieces of the smashed windshield off the bloody seat, slipped behind the wheel, changed the gear into park, and turned the key. Snow blowing in through the gaping hole not only made it difficult to see, it would also make it impossible for the heater to warm the car. To Sammy, these were just minor inconveniences in his unplanned escape from prison. Without a glance in his rearview mirror, he pulled away from the two bodies he had dragged to the ditch.

Now where could he go? Even with four-wheel drive, the van was struggling with the snow. It was just a matter of time before he was stuck, and then what would he do? A snowplow going in the opposite direction made the decision for him. In a few seconds, he had made a U-turn and fell in behind it. Wherever the plow was going, that's where he was going.

Snow blowing in through the hole in the windshield was blinding him. Visibility was almost zero, landmarks were snow covered, and even though Sammy was familiar with the town, he had no idea where this trip was going to end. Where could he hang out to plan his next step?

For a few brief seconds, the storm abated, and an elated Sammy got his bearings. He knew where he was! The snowplow was clearing a very familiar road on the peninsula. Vineyards are on the peninsula, and Sammy was well acquainted with one of them. That's where Smothering Sarah lived, or at least she used to. He was immediately engrossed with the memory of his last days of living in her house. Anger rose fresh as he recalled the night when his plan to murder Sarah had been foiled by Albert sneaking her out the window of her locked bedroom. He had no doubt that stupid Clarence had a hand in the escape, but he wasn't able to stick around long enough to find out. If his plan had worked, today he would be the owner of a successful vineyard instead of where he was now, an escaped prisoner in a bloody, windowless prison van. The indignity of being caught with his pants around his feet when the damned dog caught up with him hadn't been forgotten, either. He could still see the paper's headline the next day that the guards at the jail couldn't wait to show him: SAMMY THE GRUNT BROUGHT DOWN BY LAXATIVES AND A MONGREL DOG.

Enraged by the memories, he almost missed Sarah's driveway.

CHAPTER 6

CLARENCE WAS HAVING trouble catching his breath. He had no memory of ever walking through such thick snow. Every time he stopped for a rest, he looked around for a light, any light. The whole world was jet-black.

What if he hadn't walked in a straight line? How long could he keep this up? He'd really feel stupid if he gave up and froze to death within sight of the house. That thought gave him the incentive to keep moving toward his home.

His home. Just thinking the words made him smile. As a child, he was shuttled from one foster home to another, never living in one house long enough to make it feel like home. But now, living with Albert and Sarah was the best thing that had ever happened to him. After Sammy the Grunt, the leader of the gang he and Albert had belonged to, went to prison, and he and Albert had paid society for their crimes, the community had accepted the two of them. One of the local churches had hired Albert as their organist, and every Sunday found Clarence in that same church, dressed in his finest, ushering worshipers to their seats. Albert and Sarah had married, and Baby Paul was just icing on a cake that was already delicious. Life was good.

With the flaps pulled tight over his ears, he wasn't aware of an approaching vehicle until he was surprised by the sight of headlights in the distance. He'd walked toward the road? That was completely opposite of what he thought he was doing. As the noise got nearer,

Clarence identified the vehicle as a snowplow. His nearest neighbor, an employee of the town's road commission, was probably plowing his way home for the night.

Now that he knew where he was, he was turning in the direction that would take him back to the house when he noticed the headlights of a car following the snowplow. He watched as the car left the plowed road and turned into the driveway that led to the house.

Sarah and Albert were getting visitors on a night like this? Clarence changed directions quickly to follow the car's tracks that would take him home.

Exhausted, Clarence arrived at the dark house. Whoever it was that had driven down the driveway and left tracks for him to follow had probably saved his life. Clarence wanted to throw his arms around whoever it was, and maybe even shed a thankful tear on that person's shoulder.

Suddenly, he stopped. Why was the house dark? Even if the power was out, he knew there were candles in the house. Wouldn't a fire in the fireplace throw some light? Trudging on through the snow, the closer he got to the vehicle, the more puzzled he became; what was a, p-r-i-s-o-n, he spelled, van doing in the driveway? Pleased with himself for figuring out the word but alarmed by its presence, he paused by the van and tried to look in. Was that snow on the seat? Why would there be snow inside the van? Looking around to make sure he was alone, he reached out and pulled on the handle.

The dome light shone down on a front seat where the snow that had blown in from the missing windshield had partially covered pieces of glass, pine needles, and blood that was so fresh, it was still wet. Staggering back, Clarence pushed the van's door closed to shut off the dome light, but not forcefully enough to make a noise. It was no officer of the law who had driven this van to the home of Sarah and Albert.

Shivering, Clarence paused to think. It had been the promise of heat from the fireplace that had kept him going, but before he could go into the house, he had to find out if the people inside were in danger. And if they were, he realized that he might be the only one to save them. That thought made him stop to catch his breath. Could he save his family if he had to? All his life, people had treated him as if he were a child, and he had acted accordingly. If he was ever to grow up, now was the time.

Even in the dark, he was able to see the path that feet had made in the snow leading away from the van. Falling snow was quickly filling in the tracks to the front door. Whoever had driven the bloody prison van with the missing windshield was already in the house.

Walking around in the dark and looking into windows was not telling him anything. Working his way back to the front window, he reeled back in shock as the flare from a struck match briefly revealed the face of a man he'd hoped he'd never see again: Sammy the Grunt.

Sammy the Grunt? Clarence remembered that after Lucky, a dog mistreated by Sammy, had run the man down in Sarah's vineyard, Sammy had been sent away with a long prison sentence to federal prison. What was Sammy doing in Sarah's house?

When the burning match touched the wick of a candle, it produced enough light to reveal other people in the room. Clarence cried out in protest as Albert pushed Sarah and howling Baby Paul behind him, away from the gun Clarence could see in Sammy's hand.

Fearful that Sammy had heard him, Clarence dropped to his knees, praying that the sound of the storm and the shrieking baby had covered his cry. Relieved when nothing happened, he slowly stood up and peered into the room, only to find it dark and empty of people. Plowing back through the deepening snow, his fear allowed him to make another trip around the house, looking into every window. Where had Sammy taken the little family?

He was peering once again into the front window when his legs crumpled and his world went dark; his face landed on a pair of boots.

CHAPTER 7

ALBERT'S EYES TWITCHED, and then slowly opened. Not being able to put what he was seeing into perspective, he closed his eyes and tried to slide back into darkness. It was the voice close to his ear urging him to wake up that finally brought him to full consciousness.

"For God's sake, open your eyes!"

He could barely hear Sarah's voice over Baby Paul's piercing cry. And why was his head throbbing?

"Sarah," he mumbled. "My head hurts."

"Please, Albert, open your eyes!"

Reality hit Albert when he tried to touch the back of his pounding head and found that he couldn't; his hands were cuffed behind his back. "What the…," he yelled, fully awake.

With both eyes open, he looked around the room, trying to make sense out of what he saw. Sarah, also handcuffed, and howling three-month-old Paul were lying beside him on the floor. They were in the master bedroom, the room Sarah had refused to go into for years. It was in this room that, years before, Sammy had kept her prisoner while he schemed to become the owner of her vineyard.

"We're in trouble," Sarah whispered.

Albert's eyes swept the room. "Where's Sammy?"

"He said he had to take care of something outside."

"Sammy the Grunt!" Albert shook his head. "Ouch, that hurt! The last thing I remember is walking into this room. Is that when he knocked me out?"

"Yes. He hit you over the head with the butt of his gun." Leaning down, she squinted to get a better look at the back of Albert's head. "That's quite a bump you have. It's still bleeding, but I can't do anything about it."

Albert grimaced. "He's the last person in the world I'd have expected to show up here in the middle of a snowstorm. Wonder how many people he killed to get that uniform?"

Sarah suppressed a shudder. "We're on our own, isolated from help of any kind. This isn't good, Albert."

"Maybe our one hope is Clarence." Albert made a face. "That's a scary thing to think about!"

The raging storm was louder than the baby's cry. "Listen to that wind," Sarah shivered. "If Clarence is lost out there, he's in trouble, too. But what if he does make it to the house? How could he help us?"

"If Sammy finds him first, Lord only knows what he'll do to him. The only reason he allowed Clarence to stay in his gang was because of me."

"Clarence is a simple man, but I think he's smarter than he lets on."

Albert almost chuckled, but considering the situation, he didn't. "I've gotten him to the point of sounding out words. Wanna bet I have him reading before long?" The two grew silent, wondering if there was a future ahead for them.

It had been a dog that had figured out that the handyman Sarah had hired to work in her vineyard was the much hunted Sammy the Grunt. The federal agents had moved quickly, and Sammy never had a chance to punish Albert, who had become quite fond of Sarah, for ruining his chance to own the vineyard. Another thing he would have found out was that the stories Albert had told about his past evil deeds were just that…stories.

Sarah was remembering how frightened she'd been in this very room. She'd finally accepted her fate, said her final prayer, and then waited for Sammy to rush into the room with his knife. Being in the same room brought back unwanted memories. The grating sound of the key as Sammy had turned it to lock them in was all too familiar, part of a recurring nightmare.

Wanting to get her mind away from those memories, she turned to Albert. "Do you remember Sammy carrying the baby?"

Albert shook his head. "Sammy was behind me, poking a gun in my back. He carried Paul up the stairs?"

"Yes, he did. I hate the thought of that evil man touching my baby!"

Their crying baby was making enough racket to cover the noise of the door being unlocked and thrown open. Clarence's body came flying into the room, followed by the grinning Sammy the Grunt.

CHAPTER 8

CASTING A WORRIED look at the blackening sky, Molly ushered her buyers out the door. Heavy snowflakes, the forerunner of many if you could believe the weather report, landed on her arm as she waved goodbye.

The sudden bolt of lightning followed by the crash of thunder chased Molly back into the office. She was still standing in the middle of the room, rubbing her arms, when the phone rang.

"Hello, Allen Real…"

"Honey, it's me!" her husband, Detective Mitch Hatch, cut in. "I think you should close the office and start home. The weather is getting pretty wild."

"Did you hear the thunder? I swear the lightning must have struck near here!"

"Close up, please! Go home! The noise is scaring the twins."

"Where's Agda?"

"Ha! She's worse than the twins!"

Molly laughed. "Don't they have snowstorms with lightning and thunder in Sweden?"

"Must not! I don't want you out on the roads, either. So lock up, and go home! If Clara's there, send her home, too."

"Clara took her buyer to lunch. After that, she plans on going home. The carpenters are supposed to be finished with the addition to their house today."

Mitch chuckled. "How many people would build an addition for their dogs?"

"I know Clara was disappointed when she couldn't sell her own house so that they could buy a bigger one. The addition gives them the room they need." Molly glanced over to the corner where a huge dog bed took up a good portion of the room. "I got so used to seeing Lucky asleep on his bed, I'm rather shocked when I look and he's not there. Now that he has Lady and the pup to keep him company at home, he doesn't howl when Clara and Joe leave."

"It's really snowing hard! Please, finish up at the office and go home."

"I'll start home as soon as I do the paper work on the sale I made today. Won't take me but a minute."

"Hon, please drive careful…."

Another lightning strike followed by loud thunder left Molly with a dark office and a dead phone in her hand.

The thought of doing the finishing work on the newly sold house vanished. Maybe Mitch was right; she should lock up the office and head for home. She grinned at the thought of their Swedish au pair, Agda, being scared of the thunder and lightning. Agda had been added to the Hatch household to help Molly take care of the twins and Mitch's two nieces.

Not wanting a surge of electricity to fry the office equipment when the power came back on, Molly made a pass through the office, unplugging everything. The morning weather report had warned of a chance of snow; she had dressed appropriately. A chance of snow? What she saw out the office window was much more than "a chance of snow". Scraping snow off her car windows wasn't a task she ever looked forward to doing, but like every northern Michigan driver, she was well prepared to do it. Also equipped with snow tires and four-wheel drive, Molly's car easily swung out of the snowy parking lot.

Annoyed by distant flashing lights, she slowed down to a crawl, expecting to see nothing more than a car being towed out of the ditch. A police officer detached himself from a group, held up his hand, and brought her to a complete stop. Bundled up in his police-issued overcoat, she failed to recognize her brother, Officer Tom Allen, until she rolled down the window and he stuck his red head into the car.

"Mol, what in hell are you doing on the road in this weather?" Tom barked.

"Oh, it's you! I didn't recognize you in your winter finery. You should be home with Marie and Baby Logan."

"I hate to think of her all alone with no power and no phone, but this is my job, Mol."

Pointing at the roadblock, she asked, "What's going on?"

"What's going on is not good. The snowplow has unearthed two bodies."

"Dead bodies?"

"Very dead bodies. One of them is missing his clothes, but the other one is wearing a prison guard's uniform. There's no prison vehicle, but along with the bodies, there are large pieces of a shattered windshield and the bloody top of a pine tree. It looks like someone in the guard's clothes, including his boots, drove it away."

"Good heavens! What does the warden at the prison have to say?"

"We've been trying to call, but the storm has done away with landlines, and cell phones aren't working, either. So we don't know if they were alone, or if they were transporting a prisoner."

"If there was one, wouldn't the prisoner be cuffed and hooked to the van's security bars?"

"You got that right, Mol. Houdini would have had trouble getting out of those restraints. But get out of here and go home before the snow gets any deeper."

CHAPTER 9

"JOE, TELEPHONE!"

"Be right there, Clara," Joe called from the back of the house. "With my luck, it's probably the fire station calling me back to work."

"They'd call the chief back to work on the first day you've had off in two weeks? They wouldn't dare!"

Joe entered the kitchen chuckling. "You know better than that, dear wife. Mmmm. What smells so good?"

"The dinner that you probably won't be around to eat," Clara complained.

Hugging his petite and almost new wife, Joe took the phone. "Hello?"

Clara watched the smile vanish from her husband's face. "Wow!"

"Bad news?"

Joe nodded his head.

"I'll be there as soon as possi…hello? Hello?"

"What just happened?"

"The line went dead while I was talking to Dave. He was surprised we still have power. Seems most of the town's dark."

A flash of lightning, the crack of thunder, the sound of two huge dogs and one puppy howling…and then darkness.

"Well," Clara mumbled, "guess we're gonna find out if our new really expensive generator that I told you not to buy works."

The lights in the house came back on.

Joe looked pleased with himself. "I counted fifteen seconds before the generator kicked on. Now, are you going to apologize to me?"

"Ha. That generator is going to have to run for a couple of days before you can convince me that we didn't waste money buying it."

Joe looked out the window at the neighborhood. "We're the only house in our block with lights. Wanna bet we're going to have company before this is over?"

"Probably, and that's okay. It's going to get pretty cold in those houses real quick. But, come on, Joe, you're the fire chief. They haven't called you back to work just because the power went off."

"Well, partly. The traffic lights aren't working, plus," and here Joe mumbled something, hoping Clara wouldn't notice and ask about what she couldn't hear.

"Plus what? And please don't mumble this time. I'm on to your tricks."

Joe threw up his hands in defeat. "It appears the snowplow uncovered two bodies."

Clara nodded, encouraging him. "Go on, Joe. There's more. You aren't getting out that door until I hear the whole story."

"You are a mean woman," he chuckled, pulling her close for another hug. "I'll tell you what I know if you'll promise me that you won't let the boys eat my portion of whatever it is that's smells so good."

"I promise."

"The bodies appear to be guards from the local prison. That account is based upon the fact that one of the dead men was dressed in a guard's uniform. The second man was almost nude, but since two empty pistol holsters were found, it's a good chance that he was also a guard. Someone wearing his uniform and boots drove away in the prison van."

"With two guns?"

"Yes, and two pairs of handcuffs."

"What does the prison warden have to say about this?"

Joe shrugged. "The storm has caused a lot of problems, including knocking out landlines and a few cell towers. The warden is out of contact."

"So, if there was a prisoner in the back seat, where is he now?"

"Probably still shackled in the van, wherever it is."

"They aren't thinking that the prisoner stole the van?"

"How could he? The back door of the van can't be opened from the inside. Anyhow, prisoners are not only cuffed hands and feet, they're also chained to the van itself. No, if there was a prisoner in the back seat, he's still there."

"I still don't see why the men on duty at the fire station think you have to be there, too. Can't they handle a fire if one should happen?"

"Several of the men have been assigned plow duty. They're out trying to keep the roads open, so that leaves the station short-handed."

"Well, the snow is coming down so fast that pretty soon it's going to be impossible to drive. Are you sure our old van will make it?"

"I have new snow tires and four-wheel drive. I'll make it, but I think we should let the dogs out before it gets any deeper. Buddy has never had to deal with this much snow in his short life. He's such a character! I want to see what he does when he sees snow taller than he is," Joe laughed.

Clara headed for the stairs. "Lucky and Lady are in the addition, and the three boys have Buddy upstairs with them. The boys will want to watch the pup's reaction to the deep snow, too."

The new addition had been the answer to the housing problem caused by Lucky finding a willing stray female who'd produced two puppies. They'd kept the male puppy and had given the female puppy to Detective Mitch's nieces. The housing market in the small western

Michigan town was so depressed that even Clara, the best realtor in town, couldn't find a buyer for their old house.

As Clara got closer to the room where the three boys and Buddy were, her trouble antenna alerted her; it was far too quiet. Upon opening the door, she was assaulted by feathers that were flying out of a pillow Buddy was shaking.

"Not another pillow!" she cried. "Boys, where are you? You're supposed to be watching the pup!"

"Over here, Mom," called Jerry. "We just watched the neighbor's big tree fall over! You can see the roots and everything! Cool!"

Clara made her way to the window. Dusk had come early, but there was still enough light to see the tree. "Maybe taking the dogs outside is not such a good idea after all. It's pretty wild out there."

"But don't they have to go out?" worried Mackie, the oldest. "I don't mind cleaning up the yard after them, but I don't think I want to clean up after them in the house."

"Yes, they do have to go out, but we don't even know what Buddy will do when he sees all that snow. Let's do it while your dad is still here. He has to go back to the station."

The boys, Mackie and Billy from Joe's first marriage, and Jerry, the boy they adopted when no one claimed him after Joe had rescued him from a burning house, followed Clara.

"Wow!" exclaimed Billy. "Look at all those feathers!"

"Those feathers came out of your pillow. Now, what are you going to put under your head tonight when you go to bed?"

"You'll give me another pillow, won't you?"

"That's the third one he's torn up this week. You boys promised if we'd let you keep the pup, you'd train him. Looks like that's not happening. And to answer your question, Billy, I don't have another pillow to give you."

"Bummer," Billy muttered.

Joe was waiting at the bottom of the steps with the two big dogs. "It's really wild outside. The wind sounds like an angry animal."

Jerry ran up to Joe and tugged on his hand. "Dad, did you see the big tree go down? We did!"

"Trees are coming down? Let's get the dogs out before it gets any worse. Okay, gang, put on your coats, and let's see what happens!"

The bundled-up family stood together as Joe opened the door. Caught by the wind, the door ripped out of his hand and banged on the side of the house. All three dogs stopped. Buddy whined, and Lucky and Lady backed up. A lightning strike followed by a boom of thunder sent all three dogs rushing back into the room.

"Well," Joe chuckled, "wasn't that special? Now what do we do?"

Clara shrugged. "There was a reason why I had the workmen tile the dogs' addition. We'll just pen all three of them in there, because accidents are going to happen."

"Well, good luck. I'd better start for the station or I won't be able to get into town."

"This is crazy, Joe! What makes you think you'll even make it out of the driveway? Anyone who ventures out on the road tonight has to be an idiot!"

Wild pounding on the front door stopped the conversation. Joe grinned at Clara. "Want to answer the door and see who the idiot is?"

Mackie, who had won the race to open the door, was pushed aside by Molly, Clara's boss, who exclaimed, "Oh, thank God for generators!"

Behind her was a group of bundled up people and a yapping puppy.

Joe and Clara stood with their mouths open, watching a train of people enter their house. Following Molly was Agda with a twin under each arm, and nieces Kim and Laurie, struggling to keep Rosie, one of Lucky's pups, under control, brought up the rear. Clara was about to shut the door when Molly stopped her.

"Wait, there's more."

"More? How can there be more?"

"It's me" called Marie, "your kid sister! Did you really think I'd stay in a cold house with Baby Logan when I know my sister has a nice warm house with lights and flushing toilets? Not on your life!"

"I suppose you brought your three-pound-pampered-pedigreed-play-dog with you?"

"Leave Syndee behind? I don't think so!"

"And both of your husbands, Detective Mitch and Officer Tom? Are they coming, too?"

"Maybe later. Right now, they're working on the mystery of two dead guards and a missing prison van. You know all about this, Joe?"

"Yes, I do. Are they still thinking that the prisoner, if there was one, is still chained to the van?"

"Until the phones are back working, that's all they have to work with. We saw both our husbands at the roadblock, so they know where to find us. The town is shut down; there's no traffic and the snow is about eighteen inches deep already."

"How in the world did you get here?"

"We followed a plow. But the plows are being called off the road because even they are getting stuck. The word is that if you are home, stay at home. Hmmm. Something smells good. Could it be dinner?"

"Yes," admitted Clara, "but unless one of you can bless it and make it multiply, there's no way it's going to feed this crowd."

Molly turned to Joe. "Would you be a dear and run out to the van? Marie and I packed up the food from our refrigerators and cleaned out our freezers too. We have enough food for many days."

"Many days?" groaned Clara. "What makes you think you'll be here for many days?"

Joe was halfway out the door when Marie called out to him. "Would you please bring in the suitcases, too?"

Clara made a strangling sound. "Suitcases?"

"The heavy snow has brought down electric lines. Word is that power won't be restored for days. But don't worry about where we're going to sleep. We all brought sleeping bags. We'll just sleep on the floor. Kinda like a big sleepover party. It'll be fun!"

CHAPTER 10

ALBERT AND SARAH looked on in horror as Clarence's body slid across the floor.

Choking back a sob, Sarah whispered, "Is he dead?"

Sammy cackled, "Not yet. Maybe later?"

"What did you do to him," Albert asked through clenched teeth.

"What did I do to your little buddy? Knocked him over the head is what I did." Sammy sounded pleased with himself. "I have a small problem. Seems I'm short a pair of handcuffs, so I'll just have to keep Clarence out of commission by banging him on the head every once in awhile…unless pretty Sarah can tell me where I can find some duct tape?"

Sarah shook her head.

Three-month-old Paul, who had cried himself to sleep, chose this moment to wake up. Hungry, wet, and cold, he filled his lungs with air and howled.

Sammy covered his ears with his hands. "You shut the kid up, or I will!"

"He's hungry, and probably needs his diaper changed, too," Sarah stated quietly, trying not to sound as distraught as she felt.

A look of confusion briefly appeared on his face. "What do you feed the kid? He ain't got no teeth."

Sarah held back a surprised retort. Finally, she asked, "Sammy, have you ever been around a baby?"

"Can't say that I have."

"The only food a baby consumes for the first several months of its life is milk."

"Well, that's easy, then. I'll go down and get some out of the refrigerator. Need a cup, too? I'll bring one when I come back with the milk."

"A baby can't drink out of a cup! Anyhow, Paul is being breast fed."

The blank look on Sammy's face was replaced with a look of disgust. "You feed the baby out of your tits? What are you? A cow? That's disgusting!"

"That's how it is, so get used to the idea. He needs a clean diaper, too. Have you ever changed a baby's diaper?"

"No, and I'm not starting now."

"Then you'll have to take off my handcuffs so I can do it."

"It's getting really cold in here. What do you intend to do about that?" Albert inquired.

Sammy whirled and grabbed Albert's shirt collar. "Questions! Stop with the questions! I didn't have time to plan for all of this."

"Better start planning. We'll freeze to death up here. Are you going to feed us? What about keeping the baby warm? Have you thought about that?"

Sammy sputtered. "Keep it up, big mouth, and I'll solve all those problems by doing away with the whole bunch of you!"

"Not me, Sammy."

The quiet voice came from the corner of the room where Sammy had deposited the unconscious Clarence.

"Ah, he speaks! Guess I didn't hit him hard enough."

"You want to kill the whole bunch of them? I'll help."

"You? Help me? Clarence, you ain't smart enough to help me do anything. What in the hell are you talking about?"

"I can help you. No, it's more than that. I *want* to help you."

Albert and Sarah exchanged puzzled glances.

"I suppose you're going to tell me why? Do I need a handkerchief to wipe my tears?" Sammy cackled.

"No one knows how bad those two terrible people treat me. They've made me into a slave. If they had a dog, they'd treat it better than they treat me."

Sammy raised his eyebrows. "I'm supposed to believe that?"

"Believe what you want, but I'll prove it to you!"

Still a little shaken from the blow to his head, Clarence pulled himself off the floor, staggered over to Albert and cuffed him on the back of the head. Holding up his hand that was red with Albert's blood, he grinned at Sammy. "Want me to do it again?"

Sarah's mouth hung open. What in the world was Clarence up to? When he turned toward her, one of his eyes twitched. Was he winking at her?

"Hey Sammy, want to see what a milk cow looks like?" Grabbing the top of Sarah's dress, he ripped it open, exposing a swollen milk-dripping breast.

"Do you like this? Wanna touch it? And the screaming baby, want me to pinch him? I'll be more than happy to do that! Little shit cries all the time, anyway, so I might as well give him something to cry about. It will be fun paying back both of them for making me live in the shed. Ever since they married and got that kid, they don't want me in the house." His voice and face changed as he mimicked Sarah. "Albert and I need our privacy. Life would be *so* much better if you weren't around, so go live in the shed. Oh, yes, pruning starts at 6:00 tomorrow morning. If you plan on ever eating again, be there."

Sammy chuckled. "Interesting! So, my new little helper, make the baby shut up. He's giving me a headache!"

Stooping down, Clarence roughly picked the crying baby off the floor and carelessly tucked him under his arm as if he were a loaf of bread.

When Sarah protested, he ignored her. "Why don't we all go downstairs? Let's make a fire in the fireplace. No reason for all of us to freeze to death."

"What is that I smell?" complained Sammy. "Smells like an outhouse!"

"The kid shit. Since we'd better keep the handcuffs on Sarah, I'll take care of it. Unlock the door and keep the gun pointed at Albert. He's dumb enough to try something. Ha! I hope he does so you can whack him again!"

Albert glanced over at Sarah who was struggling to fasten her dress with her handcuffed hands. Whatever Clarence was up to, it had to be better than doing nothing.

CHAPTER 11

BY THE SILENCE in Joe and Clara's house, the assumption would be that everyone was sound asleep. The assumption would be wrong. Sleeping bags, lined up head to toe and toe to head, filled the family room, and spilled over into the kitchen. Outside, the storm roared and the generator purred. Inside, the inhabitants were snug and warm.

So who wasn't sleeping?

Buddy, one of Lucky and Lady's pups, was quietly walking among the sleeping lumps. The smells were quite interesting. Especially the shoes.

Quietly picking several of the best smellers, Buddy dragged them, one by one, into the new addition and lined them up. Buddy needed to chew. His baby teeth were falling out, and the new teeth coming in hurt. Chewing made them feel better, so Buddy chewed.

Dawn found him tired. Dawn also found him viewing his night's work with a feeling of apprehension. Remembering what had happened after he had chewed Clara's new shoes, he very carefully picked up each shoe and parceled it out to other dogs. His mother, Lady, was sleeping so quietly that she didn't stir when he deposited a heavy shoe by her side. Officer Tom Allen would have a fit in the morning when he couldn't find one of his shoes. Buddy's dad got Joe's house slipper, his sister got Baby Logan's tiny shoe, and the three-pound-pretend dog, Syndee, didn't get anything. Buddy didn't like the little yappy dog. The only shoe Buddy wanted, but didn't get, was still tied onto Detective Mitch's foot. Mitch had been so tired when he finally made it to the warm house, he had fallen asleep fully dressed, shoes and all.

The smell of bacon and brewing coffee woke several of the sleeping lumps. "Please don't tell me it's morning already," moaned one of them.

"Afraid so." The answer came from a sleeping bag near the kitchen.

Molly stuck her head around the doorway. "Mitch, are you awake?"

"Coffee! I need coffee!" called a headless sleeper from the depths of a sleeping bag.

Mitch threw off his bag and sat up. "Yes, I'm awake. Need help in the kitchen?"

"No. Marie, Clara, and I have breakfast under control. We were just wondering how you and Tom managed to get here in the middle of the night."

"Wasn't easy!" The voice came from under Tom's pillow.

"We got at least three feet of snow yesterday," Mitch explained. "The only thing able to get around in it was an earth moving machine from the construction site on Elm Street. I don't know the name of the thing, but it has treads like a tank."

"And that's how you got here?"

"Yeah," answered Mitch. "I know the guy operating it."

Tom mumbled, "It's another example of it's not *what* you know, it's *who* you know."

"You complaining?" Mitch asked with a chuckle in his voice.

Tom's voice from under the pillow sounded muffled. "You weren't the one who didn't fit into the tiny warm cab."

Molly teased her brother. "Tom, do I understand that Mitch and the driver rode in the warm cab while you froze your behind hanging on the outside?"

"You got that right." Tom sighed and rolled over. "But it was worth it just to get here. All I can say is thank God for generators!"

Joe had come down from his bedroom. "Would you please say that loud enough for Clara to hear? She had a fit because it was so expensive. It's going to have to run for several days before I expect to get an apology from her."

"I'm curious," Mitch confessed. "What keeps the generator going? What does it run on?"

"Propane," answered Joe. "We heat and cook with propane, and the generator is hooked up to the tank. I thought about going with a gasoline one, but unless you keep gas stored in your garage, getting to a gas station to fill a can would be impossible in an emergency like this. When the power went off, I counted fifteen seconds before the lights came back on."

Molly thought a bit, and then she asked, "Mitch, should we be thinking about getting our own generator?"

Mitch grinned and shook his head. "As long as we have Joe and Clara, we don't need our own."

Joe recognized the groan that came from the kitchen; it was Clara.

Commotion from the boys' upstairs bedroom caught the adults' attention. Kim and Laurie, Mitch's nieces, had chosen to sleep on the floor of the boys' room, but by the sound of things, no one was asleep.

"Oh, no!"

"Yuck!"

"Who did it?"

"I'm telling!"

Joe went to the bottom of the stairs and called up, "Need help up there?"

Silence.

Mitch joined Joe. "Laurie, wanna tell me what's going on?"

"Uh, Uncle Mitch, would you ask Joe if there's a plunger up here?"

"A plunger?"

"Yeah. Somebody plugged up the toilet."

Joe looked alarmed, "Is water running over the side of the bowl?"

"Kinda."

"What do you mean, kinda?"

"Ah, what's running over the edge isn't all water. Yuck! I just stepped in it!"

Mitch and Joe raced up the stairs. The next 'yuck' heard coming down the stairwell was uttered in a bass voice.

The clamor woke the twins, whose cries woke Baby Logan.

"I'll get him," Tom yelled to Marie who was in the kitchen.

The pounding on the door had been going on for some time before it was heard over the din. When Marie finally realized someone was at the door and opened it, she was knocked off her feet by dogs...big dogs, small dogs, and one pretend dog...that ran past her and the man who had been doing the pounding. Reaching down, the man pulled Marie to her feet and together they watched as the dogs screeched to a halt when confronted by three feet of snow. Recognizing the benefit of the path the visitor's feet had made, the bigger dogs, Lucky and Lady, relieved themselves in his tracks. The puppies followed suit, but Syndee, the pretend dog, ran back inside the house, hunkered down, and piddled on the floor.

"Breakfast is ready!" yelled Molly from the kitchen.

"We have company," Marie called out to no one in particular.

Clara headed for the door. "Who in the world is out and about on a day like…"

"Watch out for the puddle!"

"What pudd…?"

Clara's yell when she hit the floor brought Joe to the top of the stairs. "Are you all right?" he called down to his wife.

Slowly picking herself up, Clara rubbed her hip. "Gee, I bet that's gonna hurt."

Joe looked confused. "What do you mean by that? Don't you know if you're hurt?"

"Before my first cup of coffee? I don't think so!"

"Anyone know our visitor?" Marie cut in.

Mitch pushed Joe aside. "Good morning, Stan! What's happening out there in the real world?"

"Nothing is happening," Stan called up to him. "The snow is heavy; the regular plows are having trouble opening the roads."

"How about power? Has anyone gotten it back?"

"This whole section of the state is dark. It'll take days, maybe more than a week to get the power back on for everyone. Other states are sending crews to help."

A harried-looking Molly stepped out of the kitchen. "Breakfast is getting cold!" she complained. "Where is everyone? Oh, we have company?"

Joe and Mitch hurried down the stairs. "Stan is the friend who brought us home last night," Mitch explained.

"And I'm here to take you back into town, if that's what you want to do."

"There's one more guy who probably should go into town. Can your vehicle handle all three of us?" asked Mitch, trying to be heard over the cries of Baby Logan and his own twins. He threw up his hands. "It's chaos in this house!"

Stan grinned. "But it's chaos in a warm place with lights and all the other neat stuff that no one else has."

"We have to finish cleaning up a mess in the bathroom, take showers, and get dressed. While you wait, does a hot breakfast sound good to you?" Joe asked. "I'm Joe Skinner, the fire chief."

"This your house?"

Joe nodded.

"Congratulations on being smart enough to prepare for an emergency like this. Buying the generator has to be one of the best moves you've ever made," Stan remarked.

"Did you hear that, Clara?" Joe laughed. "Should I have our guest repeat what he just said?"

"I heard it the first time," Clara grumbled.

The three men left to shower and change, while the rest headed for the kitchen.

"About time," complained Molly. "I was about ready to throw it all out."

The noise level diminished as people waited their turn to fill their plates with eggs, bacon, and pancakes. Those who couldn't find a place at the table pushed aside the sleeping bags, and sat on the floor.

The peaceful setting was shattered by Tom's cry of frustration. "I can't find my other shoe!"

Marie spoke up. "It must run in the family. Logan is missing a shoe, too. They've got to be here some place in this mess of sleeping bags."

"Will you please help me find my shoe?" Tom asked his wife. "I want to eat something before we take off for town."

"You go eat, and I'll look."

Joe looked up from his freshly scraped clean plate. "That's funny. I'm missing a slipper."

Clara glanced over at her husband. "Do you think…?"

"I'm thinking Buddy," Joe nodded. "Let's check the dogs' area."

Curled up in a tight ball, sound asleep, Buddy was the only dog that looked innocent. Tom's police-issued chewed shoe lay beside Lucky. Lady had her head resting on pieces of Joe's slipper, and Rosie was curled around Logan's tiny mauled shoe.

"I don't believe this," exclaimed Clara. "Lucky has never chewed up a thing in his entire life! Why would he start now?"

Looking pained, Joe added, "And Lady! She has been the best-trained dog of them all. This is so unlike her."

"Do we punish them all?" Clara asked as she picked up what was left of Tom's shoe. "Oh, look at that!"

"Look at what?"

"Buddy, that little sneak! He left a baby tooth behind."

Joe studied the small, sharp puppy tooth sticking out of the leather. "You think Buddy is the chewer? He looks so innocent."

"I think we have a very smart puppy. He looks innocent because he made the other dogs look guilty."

Joe sighed. "Something tells me that Officer Tom is not going to be amused."

CHAPTER 12

CLARENCE BOWED HIS head and silently prayed. In his hand, he held what might be the difference between life and death for the baby.

Sammy blew on his cold hands. "Come on, dummy! I'm freezing!"

"Please, let Albert do this," Clarence pleaded. "I've never, *ever*, made a fire in the fireplace. That's Albert's job."

"Well, I guess you just got promoted. What can be so hard about starting a fire?"

Clarence clutched the book of matches Sammy had found in the guard's pocket. To survive, the baby needed the warmth from the fire, and he had just three matches to make that happen. What if he failed? He tried to keep his eyes away from the small bundle lying unattended on the floor. Hungry, cold, and needing a diaper change, Paul had cried himself into exhaustion.

Sammy punched Clarence on the arm. "Hurry up, stupid! The stinky kid is making me sick."

With a shaky hand, Clarence ripped out one of the three matches and stared at it. What if the match burned out before the kindling caught fire? Then he would have two matches left. Then what? As if an answer to his prayer, he remembered the candle.

"Sammy, where did you leave the candle?"

"The one I dropped when the hot wax hit my hand? I suppose what's left of it is still upstairs on the bedroom floor."

Within minutes, Clarence returned from upstairs with the small remnants of what was once a long candle in his hand. Striking one match, he touched the flame to the candle's wick.

Albert waved his handcuffed hands. "Good thinking! Matches burn out, but candles don't."

Clarence spun around to face Albert. "Shut up," he hissed. "No one asked your opinion."

Albert reeled back in his chair as Clarence left. Whoa! Whatever game his little buddy was playing, he was playing it with conviction.

Holding the flame to rolled up paper, Clarence started a fire that spread to the kindling. When a big log began to flame, he relaxed; he'd passed the first test. Knowing there would be more tests if he were the one to save his family from Sammy, he took a deep, relieved breath and prayed for strength. Not all those Sunday sermons had been lost on Clarence.

Sarah and Albert, their hands now cuffed in front, huddled together around the sputtering fire. Sammy had allowed Clarence to gather coats and hats, along with covers and pillows off the beds. Clarence had also found two sleeping bags in the master bedroom closet. Fortunately, the firewood Albert had previously chopped had been stored in the garage, not outside where, by now, it would be covered by several feet of snow.

Grabbing Sarah's hair, Clarence jerked back her head and looked down on her face. "So where's the kerosene lamp?"

"Ouch!"

Clarence pulled harder, "Payback time, bitch! So where is it?"

"Look behind the basement steps."

Clarence gave one more pull on her hair before turning toward the basement door…and stopped. "It's gonna be too dark down there for me to see anything."

"Take what's left of the candle," Sarah quietly remarked. "Just be careful with it."

Sammy grabbed his arm. "You just wait a minute! I don't know if I trust you to go down there. How do I know you won't try something stupid like burning down the house?"

Whirling around, he faced Sammy. "You want me to wait a minute? Did you forget that I'm on your side? Want me to prove it? Want me to hit Albert again? Want me to pinch the baby? Tell me! Just tell me and I'll do it! Now let me go. There's not much left of the candle, and we need the kerosene lamp. I can't change the shitty kid without light."

Albert held his breath, waiting for the wrath of Sammy to come down hard on Clarence. Surprised when nothing happened as Clarence pulled his arm out of Sammy's clutches and disappeared down the basement steps, he raised his eyebrows and looked at Sarah. Was she thinking what he was thinking? Would Clarence remember that they had hidden a gun in the same area? Years ago, after he and Clarence had paid their debts to society and were released from jail, neither one had informed the authorities about the gun.

Clarence reappeared at the top of the steps with a dusty lamp in his hands. "Found it!"

A touch of the candle's flame and the lamp sprung to life. No matter how hard Albert tried to catch Clarence's eye, Clarence never dropped his guard. Whatever game he was playing, he was playing it well.

Sammy held his nose. "Now you can clean the kid. I've smelled better outhouses."

"I'll change his diaper, but I don't know how clean I can get him. We don't have water."

"What are you talking about? Of course, we have water. Just go turn on the faucet."

Sarah spoke up. "Clarence is right. We get our water from a well. With no electricity to run the pump, we really don't have water. There's probably a little still in the pipes, but not much. That also means we can't flush the toilets."

Sammy sputtered. Problems, always problems. Nothing was going as smoothly as he liked. What he needed was time to think, and time to plan his next step. It wasn't as if he had plotted and planned for this escape; it had just happened. The only good thing so far was Clarence. Without his help, Sammy's only way to control the situation would have been to kill them all. He still might have to do that before this was over. His eyes scanned the room; who could he get rid of? The tail end of something Clarence was saying caught his attention…"and for additional water, we can bring in snow and melt it by the fire." Hold on! Was stupid Clarence turning into a genius?

By the light of the lamp, Clarence knelt on the floor and changed the baby. When Sammy gagged over the smell and content of the diaper, Clarence imagined what it would be like to cross the room and rub the dirty diaper across Sammy's face. Just the thought that Sammy might hurt Paul had created feelings that surprised and scared him; never before had he loved someone so much. If he had to, he would give his life to save the baby.

Hungry and cold, Paul cried.

"Do something!" Sammy demanded.

Trying to hide her desperate need to comfort her baby, Sarah calmly stated, "He's hungry."

Sammy chided. "Well, aren't we all?"

"He's just a baby, Sammy. Let me feed him, please?"

"Anything to stop that noise! Clarence, give her the baby!"

Roughly, Clarence snatched the baby off the floor and carried him, upside down, to Sarah's cuffed arms. Tears ran down her cheeks as the baby rooted, searching for her breast, and getting angry when he couldn't find it. "Clarence, I need a little help."

With no hesitation, Clarence approached Sarah as if what he was about to do was the most natural thing in the world. Pulling her dress and undergarments away, he exposed her breast. Paul latched on, sucking greedily.

"Ugh!" Sammy shuddered. "That's the most disgusting thing I've ever seen!"

Clarence was alarmed by the look on Sammy's face. What he saw was not a disgusted look; it was a hungry look. He could remember seeing that look on the faces of prison inmates who had been separated from female company for a time.

Clarence nudged him. "Sammy, come with me to the kitchen."

Sammy, his eyes on the baby who was lustily sucking on Sarah's bare breast, didn't answer.

Clarence threw his arm around Sammy's shoulder. "We need to see about food. We're all hungry."

"Wha...?"

"Let's go."

Reluctantly, Sammy tore his eyes away from Sarah's breast and allowed Clarence to point him in the direction of the kitchen.

Sarah called out, "Look in the freezer. I made several batches of bean soup with the leftover Easter ham. Put the soup in a kettle that can be placed near the fire and then see if there are any rolls left in the breadbox."

Sarah could hear Sammy berating Clarence, informing him with very strong words that no way, no how, was Clarence going near the food.

On the night that Sammy had planned to kill Sarah, Clarence had slipped what he had thought were sleeping pills into Sammy's dinner. The plan was for Albert to rescue Sarah from her imprisonment in the locked bedroom while Sammy slept. When Sammy didn't get sleepy, Albert decided that saving Sarah was worth risking his life; he had no doubt that, if caught, Sammy would kill them both.

What really saved their lives was the internal action caused by the five laxatives, not sleeping pills, that Clarence had slipped into Sammy's dinner.

The last thing Sarah heard Clarence say to Sammy before they left the kitchen was, "If I'd known then what a bitch Sarah really was, I'd have stopped Albert that night."

With bellies full, and bladders empty, thanks to melted snow that made flushing the toilets possible, the group settled down by a blazing fire for an uneasy night.

CHAPTER 13

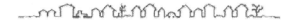

CLARA STOOD IN the doorway of her trashed family room, and sighed. Sleeping bags, open suitcases with clothes hanging out of them, empty coffee cups, and one egg-encrusted plate filled her once pristine room.

Joe, Mitch, and Tom had gone into town on the earth-moving machine with Stan. Clara had no idea who Stan was or why he was picking up the men, but he had, and he promised to bring them back at the end of the day. Until they came back tonight, there was no way to find out if the town was plowed out. Neither cell nor landline phones were working, and if any area had gotten back its power, there was no way of knowing.

From upstairs, she could hear Mitch's two nieces laughing. The Swedish au pair, Agda, was keeping them and the twins occupied. Molly was in the shower, and Marie and Logan were taking a nap. Since there were no sounds of activity coming from the addition where her three dogs, plus Rosie, and the pampered-pretend dog, Syndee were, Clara figured they were all asleep. Oh, to have the life of a dog!

She sighed again. All of this was happening because Joe had bought that generator. For the sake of her sanity, she had to believe that the electricity would come back any hour now. The emergency would be over before you knew it and, in hindsight, they could all reminisce about the great time they'd had during the big snow.

The instant response to the ringing of the doorbell was five howling dogs. Had someone gotten through the snow? No plow had shown up in this area of town. Stepping over and around the debris on her family room floor, she made her way to the front door, stood on tiptoes, and looked through the peephole.

The closest one to the door was Peggy, the mother of Molly and Tom. Clara was well acquainted with the widowed Peggy because she filled in as the office secretary when things got busy. But why was she rolling her eyes? When Peggy stepped aside a bit, Mitch's parents came into view. Mitch's mother, a retired realtor, also worked at the office doing computer work. Clara couldn't hear what Marilyn was saying to Richard, Mitch's dad, but she could see Marilyn's pointy finger waving under Richard's nose. Marilyn was upset about something. The last thing Clara noticed was the suitcases; everybody had one.

All it took to spur the five barking dogs into action was to hear the opening of the front door. They rounded the corner, streaked past Clara, and headed for the cleared area Joe had made for them.

"Wow!" exclaimed Marilyn. "That was quite a reception."

"Sorry about that," Clara declared. "Everyone okay?"

"Everyone except my cat," Richard complained.

"I told you not to bring him," hissed Marilyn.

Peggy rolled her eyes again.

Clara frowned. "You brought your cat?"

"Of course! I couldn't leave Blackie alone in that cold house. Cats get cold, too!"

Clara stepped aside. "Come on in. Oh, watch out for the do….."

The sight of five dogs running back into the house was too much for Blackie. With a hiss and a howl, he clawed his way out of Richard's arms and gave chase. The two big dogs didn't pay attention to the cat, but Syndee and the two pups took his presence as a personal affront. There was much yapping, yipping, hissing, and ripping. When they finally spotted Blackie, he was doing a balancing act on top of the rod from which Clara's new drapes flowed gracefully to the floor. Viewing the couch as a launching pad, Blackie surprised the dogs by jumping over their heads. Landing on the couch, he bounced off and headed for the stairs. The two pups and Syndee took off in hot pursuit.

Clara had watched the little scenario with a strange feeling of detachment. This wasn't really happening, was it? But there were Mitch's parents, standing in the middle of the open suitcases and sleeping bags, yelling at each other, while Peggy stood off to the side, rolling her eyes. Based on the squeals and laughter, the animals were continuing their chase upstairs.

Marilyn's voice cut through Clara's detachment. "Didn't I tell you that your cat would be nothing but trouble?"

Richard backed away from his wife. "Why should Blackie have to stay behind in the cold house? And wasn't that Tom's little dog that I just saw?"

"I still say you should have left the cat at home. Blackie isn't civilized," Marilyn shot back.

"That was a civilized dog that chased Blackie up the drapes? I don't think so."

Clara stepped between them. "No harm's been done, you two! Yes, that was Syndee. Tom's family is here, and so is your son and his family."

Richard nodded. "I thought I recognized their pup, Rosie. You already have a full house, Clara. I figured as much when I saw the car in your drive along with some strange looking tracks. If I didn't know better, I'd say they were made by a tank."

"The van is either Tom or Mitch's. Both families came in one car before the snow got too deep. As for the tracks, some guy that Mitch knows has been driving the men back and forth to work in a tank-like vehicle."

"Ha! See there, Marilyn? I was right. Are you going to apologize for laughing at me?"

Marilyn snorted.

Ignoring her, Richard explained to Clara. "It was the quest for a hot shower that made us head in your direction. When we passed Peggy's place, we stopped to see how she was making out all alone in her dark and cold house."

Peggy nodded. "I was so glad to see someone! Even though our roads are open now, the man who plows my driveway hasn't shown up yet. I couldn't have gotten here on my own."

"Well, you're all here now." Clara managed to smile at her new visitors. "How did you get here?"

Richard explained. "I asked the guy who was plowing our street where he was headed next. When he told me where he was going, I realized it was your area, so we just followed him."

"You are more than welcome; however, finding you a place to sleep is going to be a problem."

"We'll be just fine. Our sleeping bags are in the car, plus I brought stuff from my freezer and refrigerator." Marilyn turned to her husband. "Hon, when you bring in the suitcases, don't forget the spaghetti sauce! Now, where are my grandbabies?"

Clara's head was spinning. Spaghetti sauce?

"Agda is entertaining them upstairs, Molly is in the shower, and Marie and Logan are napping."

"Not anymore!" Marie called down from the top of the stairs. "What was going on down there? I heard Syndee barking."

"Your dog chased my cat up Clara's drapes," Richard chuckled.

Clara didn't.

The tangy smell of simmering spaghetti sauce filled the crowded house. Clara was tidying up the cluttered family room, Marie was off somewhere with Logan, Molly was napping with her twins, and Richard was watching the business channel on television. Agda had started a game of Monopoly with Kim and Laurie, Mitch's nieces. When Grandmother Marilyn looked over Kim's shoulder and suggested a move, Grandmother Peggy disagreed. "Do that, Kim, and you've lost the game."

"Don't listen to her," Marilyn snorted. "I've played more games of Monopoly than your Grandma Peggy has!"

"How can you say that? You have no idea how many times I've played this game!"

"Ha! I can tell! Anyone who suggested that last move doesn't know how to play the game."

"Well, I'll tell you …."

Agda interrupted. "Ladies, care to join us?"

Kim and Laurie clapped their hands.

"Scared?" Marilyn glared at Peggy.

"Scared of you? You wish!"

"Is that a yes?" asked Agda.

When both women nodded, Agda cleared the board, and a brand new game started.

With everyone occupied, the men returned home unnoticed. One step inside the door was all it took for Mitch to recognize the smell of his mom's spaghetti sauce.

"So that *was* Dad's car in the driveway! My parents are here," he remarked to the other men. "I wasn't quite sure until I smelled Mom's sauce. I don't know what she puts in it that makes it smell like that, but you guys are in for a treat!"

Marie stepped out of the den where she and Logan had been looking at books. Tom, wearing a pair of Joe's shoes, greeted his tall wife with a welcoming hug.

"What's the news from town?" she asked.

"Besides me getting reprimanded for wearing the wrong shoes?" Tom laughed. "Progress is being made. Some areas have been plowed, but not many. There's a problem of where to put the snow. There are huge piles of it already so high, it's going to be June before they're melted."

"What about power?"

Tom shook his head. "The only places open in town are the ones with generators, like the hospital and the fire and police departments. Crews are working around the clock, but the extent of damage caused by the heavy snow to lines and trees is extensive. Some roads are blocked because trees have fallen across them."

"Tom, is that your voice I hear?" called Peggy from upstairs.

"Mom, what are you doing here?" he called back.

"I could ask you the same question."

"Marie came because of Logan, and I followed Marie. Logan is the reason we needed a warm house."

"I'm here because Marilyn and Richard stopped at my house to check on me. They were on their way here for a warm shower, or so Richard claimed, and I tagged along."

Mitch spoke up. "Is my mom up there with you?"

Marilyn yelled back. "Yes, I'm here. We're in the middle of a cut-throat game of Monopoly, so quit bothering us."

Laughing, Mitch cautioned Peggy. "Watch out for my mom. She cheats."

'I'm finding that out," Peggy groused.

"Mom," Mitch called, "What made you decide to come here?"

"Well, your dad insisted we leave our cold house because of his damn cat."

"Dad brought the cat? Blackie is here? Mom, that cat is evil!"

"I know that, and you know that, but your dad doesn't. Just ask Clara how she feels about Blackie climbing her new drapes."

"Blackie did that?"

Joe cringed. Clara's new drapes had cost about as much as the generator. He had a feeling she wasn't too happy about the incident. This whole turn of events was something he and Clara had never envisioned when they'd bought the generator. Just this afternoon, three more people, plus one evil cat, had been added to the menagerie. Who was next? His musings were interrupted when he realized that Stan, the guy who had made it possible for the three of them to get into town, was talking. "…..and I promise it will be just a short shower."

"By all means," Mitch replied, sounding as if he were the owner of the house. "It's the least we can do to thank you for hauling us around. Oh, you must stay for dinner, too. You haven't lived until you've eaten my mom's spaghetti!"

"Well, if you insist," Stan agreed.

"And why not spend the night? We're all sleeping on the floor, so it's no big deal."

"Well, if you insist."

Who was next was no longer a question.

CHAPTER 14

SAMMY THREW OFF the sleeping bag and sat up. Sarah had finally gotten the baby to sleep…for the third time. If Paul was the example, when a person said that he had "slept like a baby", he was describing a night of awakening every two hours and crying.

The crying baby was not the only thing that was keeping him awake; his teeth ached. The hot soup at last night's dinner had awakened the nerves in his smashed front teeth. Man, the house was cold! After he'd tossed another log into the fireplace, he stood with his back to its warmth, studying the lumps under the pile of blankets. One of the lumps stirred. Who was going to be alive at the end of this little scenario?

His eyes found the mound that was Sarah. Despite her handcuffed hands, she was holding the baby close, sharing her body's heat with Paul. It didn't sit well with him that she was snuggling up to Albert, his former buddy. Since he had been rushed off to prison after that damned dog, Lucky, had captured him, he never did get the whole story about Albert. There had to be a reason why Albert and Sarah's dead husband were exact copies of each other. Before he did away with all of them, that's one question he'd get answered.

Strange how life had brought them together again.

After murdering an agent and stabbing a cop, he was fleeing for his life when his car had hit a deer and plunged into a ravine; he'd lost his beautiful teeth when his head hit the steering wheel. The Widow Sarah had rescued him. Her dead husband had left her a vineyard that needed constant care. Nightly she'd prayed for God to send her help; the able-bodied man she took home that night seemed to be the answer to her prayers.

For Sammy, the vineyard had been a safe place to hide. When Albert and Clarence were released from prison, they'd joined Sammy at the vineyard. When Sarah had found out who was living under her roof, she rightly feared for her life.

Rubbing eyes that were trying to close, he shook himself. He didn't have time for sleep; he needed to plan. How long before the power came back? How long before the plows opened the road? The driveway to the vineyard must have three feet of heavy snow on it by now. Who plowed the driveway? If Albert plowed his own driveway, wouldn't a neighbor notice that there was no activity at the vineyard? If someone came snooping around, how would he handle it? His head was spinning with so many questions that had no answers.

Back when he had plans to get rid of Sarah and take the vineyard for himself, Albert and Clarence had interfered; they'd become sweet on Sarah. New rage boiled up inside him. If they had allowed him finish her off, he'd be the owner of the vineyard right now. Instead, he was an escaped prisoner trapped in a cold house with no end in sight. What would happen when the snow stopped and the roads were plowed open? How long could he keep these people prisoners? What about Clarence? Could he really trust him? His story about being treated badly didn't sound too convincing. It was the strange puzzled look on Albert and Sarah's faces that gave him plenty of doubt about Clarence's accusations. Without his help, the only other way for him to stay undiscovered on the vineyard would be to eliminate everyone in the house.

Shivering, he crawled back into his sleeping bag; dare he go to sleep? His own body heat captured inside the sleeping bag was like a drug, coaxing him. Against his will, his eyes kept closing. The noise of a shift in the burning log interrupted his slide into deep sleep. He knew it was just a matter of time before his body responded to his need for rest. While he was sinking into oblivion, a flare from the burning log briefly illuminated the pile of blankets that covered Clarence. Sammy didn't have a choice; his eyes closed. He'd trust Clarence until he did something that didn't fit into his revenge story. Then he'd have to kill them all.

The day that had started out with a trip into town for a dental appointment had turned out to be so much more. This morning, he'd been a prisoner behind bars; this evening, he was a prisoner behind three feet of snow. In his heart, he knew that there wasn't a chance that the present situation was going to end well. He was, once again, a loser.

When next he opened his eyes, morning light was pouring in through the window.

Clarence was standing over him, pointing a gun.

CHAPTER 15

BUDDY WAS RESTLESS. Looking over the mounds of sleeping dogs, his eyes landed on his littermate, Rosie. One day the two of them had been rolling, biting, and pretending to kill each other, and then the next day she wasn't anywhere. He'd looked and looked for her...until he forgot about her. But here she was, and it was just as if she'd never gone away. Remembering their midnight antics, he picked his way between the two sleeping big dogs, and stood over her. When a poke with his nose didn't waken her, his sharp baby teeth gnawing on her ear did.

Together they padded silently into the main part of the house, sniffed the sleeping forms on the floor, and looked for interesting things. The result of Buddy's effective job of chewing Tom's shoe was their absence; there were no shoes to chew tonight. Rosie found a paper plate with the remains of last night's dinner still on it. Being a good sister, she shared the plate with Buddy.

Moving on, they left the sleeping lumps, heading for the kitchen. Both puppies stopped, sniffed, and then with tails wagging, ran toward a wonderful smell. The aroma was coming from the counter, way too high for the pups to jump. But wait a minute. What was that other smell? It was cat stink! And there, high up on the counter, batting a sausage link back and forth between his front paws, was Blackie the cat. With green eyes peering over the edge of the counter, he teased the puppies. He pushed the link to the edge and watched them drool and spin around, waiting for it to fall to the floor. With cat grace, Blackie played with the link until the pups were frantic. Finally, one last bat from the cat's paw flipped the link off the counter. With cat disdain, he watched as the pups tussled with each other over the prize. When Buddy ran off with it, Blackie batted another link over the edge for Rosie.

It was a fun game, but the cat quickly grew tired of it; it was time to move on. With one last bat, he pushed two open packages of frozen breakfast sausages off the counter.

The pups pounced.

Soon, the partially frozen greasy meat had made cold balls in the puppies' stomach. Buddy wasn't feeling so good. Water...he needed water. Racing for the bathroom, he passed Rosie who was making choking sounds as she headed for the living room.

Marie's scream and Buddy's yelps awakened the sleepers.

"What th...?"

"Someone vomited on my sleeping bag!"

A sleepy voice muttered, "You just had a bad dream."

"Dreams don't have chunks," Marie snorted. "And whose dog is that yelping?"

"What's going on down there?" Joe called from the top of the stairs.

"Ouch!" exclaimed a deep voice. "I just got stepped on! Would someone please find the light switch?"

"I can do that from up here," Joe announced.

Joe turned on the light in time for the newly awakened sleepers to see Lucky coming out of the bathroom carrying a dripping wet Buddy by the scruff of his neck. Picking his way around the sleeping bags, Lucky left behind him a trail of dripping toilet water.

The group watched in silence until a female voice exclaimed, "Okay, guys. Which one of you didn't put down the toilet seat?"

CHAPTER 16

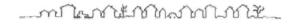

WARDEN CHARLES HAGER held the silent phone to his ear. There was still no dial tone. How many more days was it going to take to recover from the storm? The plows were making progress on the roads, but electricity hadn't been restored; neither the landline phones nor the cell phones were working. Because the prison's huge generators had kicked in immediately after a lightning strike had cut off the power, the inmates had no idea that a storm had plunged a whole section of the state into darkness.

It was the nagging "something's not right" feeling that had robbed the warden of sleep the past two nights. Not knowing the whereabouts of his two guards and their prisoner, Sammy the Grunt, was more than worrisome. He kept telling himself that the two guards were resourceful; if they had run into trouble, they'd figure out how to handle the situation. Reminding himself that the prisoner was chained securely to the van brought him moments of relief. But still....

He looked up as his secretary approached his desk.

"Warden Hager, you asked me to keep you informed on road conditions. A supply truck driver just reported that most of the roads are open. Some of them have just one lane cleared, but they're passable."

"Thank you, Jenny. Is Jim around?"

"Yes, he is. I saw him just a minute ago."

"Please send him in."

A few minutes passed before the door opened and a guard stood in the doorway.

"You want to see me, Warden?"

"Jim, how would you like to take a drive over our newly opened roads?"

"And where would I be going, sir?"

"You'd be going to look for Sammy the Grunt and two guards who started out for the dentist two days ago. Since there are no phones, the only way we can find out what happened to them is to go there. You may take another guard with you."

"When do you want this done?"

"I want you to go as soon as you find someone to go with you. Ask Jenny for the name and address of the dentist. I'm sure they've holed up somewhere to weather the storm, but I won't feel easy until I know that everything's all right."

———————

SAMMY ATTEMPTED TO sit up.

"Don't even try!" Clarence commanded.

"What th…?" Sammy blinked and shook his head. What was Clarence doing with his gun?

"Just what do you think you're doing?" snarled Sammy. "Give me back my gun. How the hell did you get it?"

"This ain't your gun, Sammy. And if you try to pull your gun on me, you're dead. Did you hear me, Sammy? Dead!"

"Ho, ho! The true Clarence shows his face! I shudda known."

"You ain't in control no more, Sammy. We are!"

"You sure are talking big, dumbhead. I'll bet that gun ain't even loaded."

"Wanna bet?"

Looking past Clarence, Sammy could see Albert and Sarah glaring down at him.

"So, what do we have here? Your handcuffed buddies here to help you?"

"They won't be handcuffed much longer. Where's the key?"

Remembering that the key to unlock the handcuffs was somewhere in the backseat of the van, he chuckled. "If I didn't have to pee so bad, I'd have a belly laugh right now."

"Go ahead and laugh. You ain't going nowhere!"

"And neither are those two. I don't have the key."

"Shit," muttered Albert. "Now what?"

"That's it?" Sarah glared at her husband. "We're going to take his word for it? Search his pockets!"

Sammy smirked. "Who's gonna do it? I see two handcuffed people and one idiot with a gun."

The truth in Sammy's assessment of the situation momentarily silenced the group. Even unarmed, Sammy still had the upper hand.

"Should I just shoot him?" Clarence asked. His hand holding the gun was shaking.

Sammy sucked in a quick breath; he'd never seen Clarence hold a gun. The simple-minded man had attached himself to Albert, and because Albert's wild stories sometimes included Clarence in the plot, Sammy had allowed him to join his gang. Come to think of it, Albert had never once lived up to his boasted violent past.

Having no doubt that Sammy wouldn't think twice about killing them all, Sarah anxiously waited for Clarence to pull the trigger. Instead, she saw his hand wavering as conflicting emotions weakened his resolve. A fierce maternal feeling to protect the baby in her arms was making her frantic. "Pull the trigger, Clarence!" she screamed. "Do it! He'd kill us without a second thought."

Clarence hesitated. Could he actually pull the trigger and end a man's life?

"What are you waiting for?" Sarah urged. "This is a no-brainer! He forced his way into our house and made us prisoners. The law allows you to kill someone who does things like that! Do it for Paul's sake!"

Words from Sunday morning sermons ran through Clarence's head. Did the commandment "Thou shall not kill" have a loophole? Would God give him a free pass on that commandment if he had to kill someone to save himself? Clarence wavered. He'd prayed for strength to save his family, and God had given him that strength, but would God be pleased if he killed Sammy?

Sarah was beside herself. "If you aren't going to do it, then, give me the gun! I'll shoot the bastard! Hold out your arms, Albert. I'm giving you the baby."

"Wait a minute," Albert argued. "If anyone's going to shoot Sammy, it should be me. Clarence, give me the gun."

"Pull the trigger or give up the gun!" pleaded Sarah. "Do it!"

Clarence closed his eyes, quickly said a short prayer asking God to forgive him, and pulled the trigger.

Nothing happened.

Dumbfounded, Clarence stood, looking down at the gun in his hand. Was this God's way of saying he wanted Sammy to live? Was he not supposed to save his family? A feeling of detachment settled over him as he watched Sammy almost free himself from the sleeping bag and lunge toward him. Behind him, he could hear Sarah yelling at him, something about shooting.

"Shoot him again!" was what Sarah was shouting. The baby she had placed on the floor was wailing, protesting the absence of Sarah's body heat.

Without thinking, Clarence obeyed Sarah's order and pulled the trigger. The explosive noise so astonished him, he was slow to realize that the bullet had whizzed past Sammy's head.

Clarence's hesitation was all Sammy needed. Ignoring the warm urine that was running down his leg, he frantically scrambled to finish untangling himself from the sleeping bag.

Reality hit Clarence; coming at him was the devil. The evil grin on Sammy's face was the last thing he saw before he tossed the gun over his shoulder and disappeared under the weight of Sammy's body. It was an uneven fight; Sammy fought dirty. With his fist raised high to deliver the final blow to an already unconscious Clarence, Sammy stopped when he felt the barrel of a cold revolver being pressed into his neck.

"Shoot him, Albert!" cried Sarah. "Shoot him while you have the chance!"

Albert tried to steady his shackled hands. Sensing a weakness, Sammy whirled around, struck the gun, and with a cry of victory, lunged after it.

"No!" screamed Sarah. Grabbing and swinging the fireplace poker with her cuffed hands, she was as surprised as Sammy when it hit his head with a resounding thunk. Sammy crumpled.

Both Clarence and Sammy were lying on the floor, unconscious. Clarence's nose was bleeding and the area around his eyes was already swollen; Sammy had blood running from a cut on his head.

Trying to steady his voice, Albert asked, "What do we do now?"

"I know where there's some duct tape. If we can tape him, maybe we don't have to kill him."

"Maybe you already did that. He hasn't moved since you hit him."

"So be it. If he's dead, he's dead. Then all of us will be safe until the power comes back on and we get plowed out."

CHAPTER 17

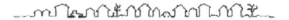

THE PRISON VAN drove slowly through the quiet town. The roads were opened, but all the stores were dark along the main drag.

"Looks like the power is still out," remarked Jim.

Bill, the guard who'd accompanied Jim on the mission, held his cell phone to his ear. "There's no phone service, either."

"Have you ever been to this town?" Jim asked.

"Never," replied Bill. "In my free time I head back south to my family. They can't understand why I stay in this frozen tundra!"

Jim grinned at him. "Come on, Bill! You know you love it."

Bill snorted as he moved the car's heater up another degree. "Just shut up and find a building that looks like a police station."

IT WAS QUIET around the breakfast table. Supplies were getting low, and without the sausage links to supplement the omelet, it had been a skimpy meal.

Marie's chair was empty. Those still at the table could hear gagging sounds coming from the laundry room. Removing Rosie's deposit of the unchewed midnight snack from her sleeping bag wasn't setting too well with Marie's stomach.

Molly pushed back her coffee cup. "I don't know how I feel about sleeping in a bag that's wet with toilet water."

"It was clean water," Mitch pointed out. "It just had a little bit of Buddy's fur mixed in it."

"How in the world did the pups get the sausage?" Clara wondered. "They certainly didn't jump to the counter…it's too high!"

Marilyn glared at her husband. "Richard, do you have something to say on the subject?"

"Me?" Richard raised his eyebrows.

"Yes, you!"

Mitch looked at his dad. "Oh, oh! What makes us think that an evil cat had something to do with this?"

Marilyn huffed, "That's because an evil cat probably had a lot to do with shoving the sausage off the counter!"

Pushing back his chair, Mitch got to his feet. "Dad, you should have left your cat at home."

Richard snorted. "Why? No one left their dog at home to freeze!"

It hit Mitch that his dad had a good point. There are dog people, and there are cat people. His dad had always loved cats. "Dad, I'm wrong; I shouldn't have said that. You love your cat and you did the right thing, so don't let Mom and me make you have second thoughts about bringing Blackie." He turned to the guys who were still at the table. "Tom, Stan, and Joe, finish your breakfast. I'd like to head for town in the next fifteen minutes."

Clara called from the kitchen. "Are the grocery stores open?"

"The big chain one is," Joe called back.

"Grab the grocery list on the way out. Feeding this many people takes a lot of food."

"Meet you at my car in fifteen," Mitch called to the other three men.

———

THE TWO GUARDS were still driving slowly through town, looking on both sides of the street for something that looked like an official building. A car going the other way caught Bill's eye. "Hey, can you follow that car? The passenger is wearing some kind of uniform."

Making an illegal turn, Jim drove the van behind the car and followed it for several blocks before it pulled to the curb and stopped. Getting out of the car were two men in uniform, and one in street clothes.

Noticing a van that had pulled in behind their car, Tom remarked, "I think we have company."

"Do you recognize them?" asked Joe.

"No, but they're both wearing some kind of uniform."

"If they aren't from around here, that means the roads have really been plowed," reasoned Mitch. "About time."

Stan stayed in the car while the other three got out and approached the van.

The uniformed driver of the van opened his door and stepped out. "We're looking for the police station."

Grinning, Tom held out his hand and stepped forward. "That's an easy one. I'm Officer Tom Allen."

Another man climbed out of the van and joined the group. "Man, it's hard to imagine what life was like back in the good old days" he laughed. "Without electricity and phones, it's just plain footwork!"

Mitch joined the conversation. "At least you didn't have to ride a horse to get here," he said as he held out his hand. "Hello, I'm Detective Mitch Hatch. The other man in uniform is Joe Skinner, our Fire Chief."

Jim took Mitch's hand. "Both of us are prison guards. I'm Jim, and he's Bill."

After the introductions, Tom asked, "May we ask why you're here?"

"The day of the big storm…three days ago…two of our guards were transporting a prisoner to a dentist here in town. We're just checking up on them."

When the smiles vanished from the faces of the three men, Bill held his breath; one of the guards was his best friend.

Hating to be the bearer of bad news, Tom swallowed a lump in his throat. "There's been an accident," he said quietly. "We have two bodies at the morgue that need to be identified."

"They're dead?" cried Bill.

"They need to be identified, but I'm sure that's who they are. One of them was wearing a uniform like yours."

"Just one had a uniform? Why just one? Both were guards." Jim placed his hand on Bill's shaking shoulder, trying to comfort him.

Detective Hatch stepped forward. "Tell us about the prisoner."

"If there was an accident that killed both guards, didn't the prisoner get killed, too?"

"There's no sign of a prisoner."

"What about the van?"

"There's no van."

Jim stepped closer. "Wait a minute! What kind of an accident are you talking about?"

"A plow clearing the road uncovered the bodies. Along with large pieces of a shattered windshield, there was the top of a bloody pine tree. Since both victims had wounds with pieces of pine remaining in them, the coroner figured a tree had crashed through the windshield."

"And the van, the prisoner, and a uniform are missing?"

"That's right. Could the prisoner have freed himself, put on the guard's uniform, and then driven off with the van?" Tom asked.

Jim shook his head. "No way! I was there when the prisoner was hooked up in the back seat of the van. I know he had cuffs on his hands and feet. There's no way in hell he could have gotten himself out of there!"

"So, you're saying that wherever the van is right now, the prisoner is still chained in the back seat?"

Jim shook his head. "Has to be!"

"Who is the prisoner?" asked Joe.

"A guy named Sammy the Grunt. He was recently transferred to us from the federal prison downstate." Jim stopped talking when he saw the startled look on the faces of the three men.

"You know the guy?" he asked.

CHAPTER 18

SAMMY WOKE TO blinding pain. His head. Something was wrong with his head. Why couldn't he move his hand to touch the place that hurt so much? And the noise! The clattering of metal on metal amid arguing voices and the cries of a baby were making him nauseated. He opened his mouth to object to the noise, but nothing happened. His mouth was so dry, his tongue was stuck to its roof. Water. He needed water. Was it just his imagination or did he actually hear splashing water?

"You did it again, Albert!" Sarah cried, pointing to the puddle on the floor. "Look at all the water you wasted."

"Can't help it! My hands are freezing!"

"I'm sorry I yelled," Sarah said quietly. "It's so hard to do anything with these stupid cuffs."

"Clarence needs to wake up."

"Let him sleep a bit longer. He needs to recover from the rough clean-up job I did on him."

"You sure had him howling!"

"Hey! With cuffed hands, I did the best I could do. Has Sammy moved?"

"Doesn't look like it. Do you think our duct tape job is going to hold him?"

"It better. When Clarence wakes up, he can check."

Albert struggled to pick up a large kitchen pot. "I'm going out for some more snow."

"All I can say is thank goodness we don't have to drink that water. We have enough beer and pop left over from Paul's christening party."

"Did you notice that it takes ten inches of snow to melt into about one inch of water?"

"I didn't know the ratio, but I was surprised to see all that snow turn into so little water. The toilet needs to be flushed again."

"That means many more trips outside!" complained Albert.

"Tell you what. I'll go out for the snow, and you go to the garage for some more wood."

"Sorry about being grumpy, hon. It's just that I feel so helpless. I'm the one who should be keeping my family safe, not Clarence."

Sarah struggled to keep the blanket from falling off her shoulders. "Damn these cuffs!" she muttered and took the pot from Alfred. "You have to admit that he surprised both of us. I think he's been playing dumb most of his life when he really isn't," she remarked as both of them headed outside.

The sound of the closing door stirred Sammy. "Water!" he croaked. "I need water."

BILL LOOKED DOWN on the dead face of his best friend. "I'm godfather to his four-year-old," he remarked quietly to the coroner.

The coroner replied, "This is never an easy job."

Jim threw his arm around Bill. "We need to get back to the prison. The warden needs to hear about this."

Jim still had his arm around Bill's shoulders when they ran into their four new acquaintances outside the building.

"Could we buy you a cup of coffee?" Mitch asked.

Bill wiped his eyes on his sleeve. "We saw the look on your faces when we told you the identity of the prisoner; we'd like to hear more about Sammy the Grunt."

Over coffee and pastries, the guards listened to the tale of the two drug murders that had sent Sammy, Albert, and Clarence to prison. Freed by technicalities, Sammy had gone back to the little town with revenge in his heart and had gotten into trouble.

"Wait a minute. Didn't the people in the town know what Sammy looked like? How'd he get away with that?" Bill asked.

Mitch picked up the story. "Sammy had worked on changing his appearance. He was an ugly-long-grey-haired-rotten-toothed man when he went into prison. No one recognized him when he came out with short blond hair, beautiful teeth, and a muscular body. With his new look, he moved around freely. He got interested in real estate for some reason. Oh, did we mention that he killed an agent on her lunch break?"

While holding his hand over a spot near his heart, Tom told how Sammy had stabbed him, and then drove his car over the side of a steep hill trying to escape. "That's how his teeth got smashed."

On the pretext of keeping their cups filled, the waitress hung around the table, enthralled by the story she was hearing. All this was going on in her little town and she hadn't been aware of it? Was she to believe that there really was a man by the strange name of Sammy the Grunt who had done all these things?

A sudden memory of a man that fit his description made her catch her breath. Since the diner held the servers accountable for the food that they served, any customer who stiffed her was etched into her brain. She remembered a man who had ordered a piece of cherry pie and a cup of coffee. He had been watching the noon news on the diners' television set when all of a sudden he had jumped up and rushed out of the diner without paying. She had been watching the news, too. Could it be? Her eyes landed on the redheaded cop at the table. Yes, she distinctly remembered the news was showing this very same cop bringing the body of the murdered real estate agent up from a ravine. Realizing she had been so close to evil made her shiver.

Rubbing the goose bumps off her arms, her attention went back to the men at the table.

"...and that's when we arrived at the vineyard and rescued Sarah."

"What a story! Who figured out that it was Sammy the Grunt who was living on Sarah's vineyard?" Bill asked.

The men looked at each other. Mitch shook his head. The dog, Lucky, had figured it out, but explaining this to the guards was too complicated. Joe threw up his hands and said, "That's the story in a nutshell."

Jim put down his cup. "What about that Sarah woman who picked him up after his accident? Is she still around?"

"She married Albert, the guy who saved her when Sammy was about to kill her," answered Mitch.

"Wasn't he one of Sammy's gang?"

"Albert had an interesting past. Turns out, he was a bad guy only in the stories that he told."

Jim pressed on. "Do you ever see them? I mean Sarah and Albert."

"Every Sunday. Their baby was christened just a few Sundays ago. Albert plays the organ at the church that most of us attend. His sidekick, Clarence, is an usher."

The men were silent while the server refilled their cups.

Joe looked up from stirring sugar into his coffee. "Could we even consider the possibility that Sammy somehow got himself out of his chains, took the guard's uniform, and drove off with the van?"

Jim shook his head. "Don't think so. But what if he did? Where would he go?"

"Maybe the vineyard?" Joe looked at his two buddies. "Think about it. He lived there for almost a year before things came to a head."

Mitch chuckled. "Joe, remember when we laughed at your wife? She was the only one who believed Lucky."

Bill and Jim looked puzzled. "Who's Lucky?"

Tom silenced Mitch with a look. "Never mind."

Jim shrugged, looked at his watch, and stood up. "Well, I think we've heard enough about Mr. Grunt. It's time to go back and report the bad news to the warden."

SAMMY WOKE UP shivering. He was freezing, his head was pounding, and his tongue felt thick. The blanket that someone had thrown over him had slipped off. Raising his head, he could see three motionless mounds next to the fireplace. That's where he needed to be.

The tape held him captive, but he could squirm, and he could roll. He even worked up a little sweat as he wriggled toward the fireplace. Exhausted when he finally got there, the warmth from the fire would have coaxed him back to sleep if he hadn't made a discovery; the tape around his hands was loose.

CHAPTER 19

"OH, NO! There he goes again."

Squinting, Joe glared at the digital clock on the nightstand. "Three o'clock! Logan's right on schedule. When do babies start sleeping through the night?"

Clara's muffled voice came from under the pillow. "Evidently he's not there yet. God, he's loud! But I was actually sleeping until you opened your big mouth."

"Oh, aren't we the jolly one, Miss Sunshine!"

"Ha! I need my sleep. You get to leave this trashed house and go out to a civilized world. I'm stuck here with in-laws, out-laws, an au pair, kids, babies, five dogs and one evil entity that pretends to be a cat."

Joe sighed. "I hate to admit this, but you were right about the generator. At this point, freezing to death is sounding better all the time. Life in a commune sucks."

Clara snickered. "You're funny, Joe. And really, the past four days haven't been that bad. To be honest, there are more good times than bad. This can't go on for much longer, can it?"

"People in part of the blacked-out area have already gotten back their electrical power. Crews from other states have been working right along with our own guys. It's just a matter of time."

"We won't know when it comes back on. Isn't that what the installer said? When the electrical power comes back, our generator just shuts off. Gee, I hope someone will tell us when that happens!"

"If it's night, we'll just see lights in other houses."

Clara had dropped off to sleep when Joe's voice woke her up. "Honey, remember when Lucky figured out that Sammy the Grunt was the handyman on Sarah's vineyard, and you were the only one who believed him?"

She sighed and rolled over. "Yeah. You all laughed at me."

"Well, I got laughed at today."

Clara sat up. "You know something! Yes, you do! What aren't you telling me?"

"We met two guards from the prison today. They were sent here to find where the other two guards and the prisoner had found shelter when the storm hit." Joe stopped talking and swallowed hard. "The scene at the morgue was most unpleasant."

Clara reached out and patted him. "So there was a prisoner?"

"Yes, there was, and does the name Sammy the Grunt ring any bells with you?"

"Oh, my God!" breathed Clara.

"Quite a shocker, isn't it?"

"Oh, my God!"

Joe chuckled. "Are you swearing or praying?"

"Both! I feel as if you hit me in the stomach. What was he doing anywhere near our town?"

"The story is that his smashed front teeth were aching and the prison dentist was in the hospital with a burst appendix. Two guards were transporting him to one of our local dentists when they ran into the storm. Sammy had nothing to do with their deaths."

"I've seen how prisoners are shackled in prison vans! There's no way he could get out of those restraints!"

"Well, if he didn't, then whoever drove off in the prison van still has Sammy."

"This is all pretty scary, but you haven't explained why they were laughing at you."

"That's because I came up with the theory that he somehow got out, put on the dead guard's uniform, and drove off in the van. And where would he go? He'd go to a place he was familiar with."

"The vineyard?" whispered Clara. "Sammy is back at the vineyard?"

"Go ahead, laugh. I laughed at you last time."

"I'm not laughing. I'm thinking about Sarah and her baby being terrorized by Sammy the Grunt."

"Well, no one took my theory seriously."

Clara threw her arms around him. "I do," she said softly. "We'll talk about this in the morning, okay? Now go to sleep."

She was making serious snoring sounds when he whispered, "Thanks for not laughing at me, hon."

CHAPTER 20

QUIETLY, LUCKY MANEUVERED his way around the sleeping Lady and her two pups, Buddy and Rosie. Syndee, the pretend dog, and Blackie, the evil cat, were nowhere to be seen. They had become more than friends; they had become partners in mischief.

It was morning, and the enticing smell of food was drifting from the kitchen. Lucky could hear murmuring coming from the sleeping bags in the living room. The new day had started, and he intended to be part of it.

For all the years he had lived with Clara, the two of them had been inseparable. She had tried to leave him home alone when she went to work, but his loud and unstoppable howling was unacceptable to the condo management and her neighbors. Lucky's refusal to ride in a car meant that Clara had to walk him back and forth to work. When Clara and Joe married, they'd bought a house that was within walking distance of both Allen Real Estate and the fire station.

Lucky's life changed the day he arrived home with a stray female along with two puppies that looked suspiciously like him. With Lady and the pups for company, he was happy to stay at home.

Lately, the novelty of staying home had worn thin; he was bored. He missed riding on the miniature fire truck that was hitched to Clara's car, and he missed the excitement of riding on the real fire truck with Joe.

The bodies from the floor were wandering into the kitchen looking for coffee. As the communal way of living stretched into days, survival of the fittest had become the order of the day; the women were no longer cooking. If too many chefs spoil the broth, then five women in a kitchen spoil the tranquility. There are many ways to solve a problem, to cook a meal, or to create a menu; each woman had a strong opinion about every one of them. The final argument that ended the cooking arrangement was over the right way to load the dirty dishes into the dishwasher. Now, when they ran into each other in the kitchen while making their own meals, they gave each other the cold shoulder and a dismissive huff. The refrigerator's interior had been sectioned off to accommodate the different families. Warning notes printed on personal food containers had messages that wouldn't look out of place in a war zone.

Each morning, after everyone had had their initial bathroom visit, they'd eat whatever was in their section of the refrigerator while waiting their turn for the shower.

Lucky moved around the room, accepting pats on the head and bits of food that were slipped to him. His eyes were on Clara. It was her car that had the hitch to attach the miniature fire truck.

After Joe and Clara's wedding, fitting everything into a working schedule had been taxing their patience. The boys' schedule they could handle; the bone of contention was Lucky. In the morning, there were heated arguments as to whose turn it was to walk him to work; the same argument arose in late afternoon with calls between Allen Real Estate and the fire station. Lucky was the reason for all the friction. Joe's fellow firefighter, Dave, had solved the problem. Since Lucky loved to ride on the big fire truck, Dave built a miniature one and mounted it on a trailer.

Lucky hung around the bathroom door. Clara was in there, and he knew that when she came out, she'd grab her car keys and head out the door to her car. While waiting for Clara, he heard the jingling of car keys and noticed that the men were putting on coats; maybe one of them would be driving the car with the trailer. They were so busy laughing and clanging things together, that no one noticed Lucky slipping out the door. There were two cars and one funny looking machine in the driveway; he was disappointed that the car with the trailer was nowhere to be seen. The car the men headed for was covered with new snow. They had brushes, and to Lucky, it looked like fun…at least the men were laughing when they threw snow at each other. He almost joined the game, but held back at the last minute. He didn't want to miss Clara when she came out.

Finally, when the car was free of snow, the men jumped in and headed for town. The roads might be open, but that didn't mean that Stan had moved on. He figured that the one invitation to spend the night was good for the duration of the blackout. No one questioned his presence.

Now that the Omelet Shop had its own generator, the men were headed there for breakfast.

Lucky was getting cold. Maybe Clara wasn't going anywhere today. In fact, she hadn't gone anywhere in several days. He'd like to get back into the house, but being out wasn't so bad. At least it was quiet. Someone complaining about being kept awake by a crying baby drowned out his halfhearted scratch on the door. Blackie and the pretend dog were up to something; the dog was yipping and a voice was coaxing the cat to come down from somewhere. Perhaps the drapes again? It was the cry from the kitchen about a missing sandwich that made Lucky turn away from the noise in time to see a truck stopping at the house next door. Two men got out of the truck and walked to the back. After they'd lowered one side of the truck's bed, both men walked up the ramp, picked up a heavy box, and jointly carried it into the neighbor's house. To Lucky, the empty bed of the truck looked as good as his trailer. Since anything was better than going back into the noisy house, he walked up the ramp, curled up in the corner of the bed, and fell asleep.

CHAPTER 21

"CLARENCE, WAKE UP," whispered Sarah.

Clarence grunted and rolled over.

"Wake up," Sarah insisted.

"Wh…?" Clarence squirmed away.

Sarah poked him harder with her toe. "Be quiet," she hissed. "Don't wake Sammy. We have to talk."

The eyes that Clarence tried to open were black-rimmed and swollen. He ran his tongue over dried-blood-covered lips. "Is it morning already?"

"Lower your voice! Yes, it's morning already. Sammy's still asleep, and let's keep it that way."

Clarence grunted. "I hurt all over."

"And you don't look so good, either." She held up her cuffed hands. "I didn't do such a great job of cleaning you."

"I'm awake, so now what?"

Sarah motioned with her head. "Let's go into the kitchen in case Sammy is faking. Anyhow, we need to come up with something for breakfast. Throw another log on the fire, and then meet me there. That's where Albert is."

"I'll be there after a stop at the bathroom."

Looking into the bathroom mirror, he grimaced at his image. Cold water from a bowl of melted snow felt good on his eyes, and when he washed away the dried blood on his lip, he saw that it wasn't a deep cut. It had been a terrifying beating, but he had survived. Squaring his shoulders, he headed for the kitchen.

Living so far out of town, Sarah always bought in bulk. Cases of canned food, powdered milk, toilet paper, and oil were stockpiled in the basement.

"That's the last of the bread," she lamented. "From now on, we eat from cans." Albert and Sarah worked well as a handicapped team. It took both of them to use the can opener; Sarah held the can while Albert turned the handle.

"So, what's up?" Clarence stood with his empty plate, waiting for his share.

Albert looked at his buddy. Sammy had beaten him within an inch of his life. The only reason he was still alive was Sarah's good aim with the poker.

"You have to go for help."

It was a blunt statement, but Clarence didn't blink. He had already come to that conclusion.

"I know you're going to ask me if I can drive the plow truck. It has a stick shift, and the answer is no, I can't drive it. I've tried, remember?"

"Without plowing the driveway, there's no way to get the car out of the garage. I have no idea about the main roads."

"Too bad our snowmobile won't work in three feet of heavy wet snow," Sarah remarked.

With a bright look on his face, Clarence exclaimed, "Didn't I see snowshoes in the basement? I think I knocked over a pair when I was down there looking for the lantern and the gun."

An unexpected voice from the doorway exclaimed, "That's good to know!"

Clarence looked around too late to dodge the poker coming straight for his head. Sammy, with yards of duct tape still hugging his body, struggled to stoop down to the unmoving body on the floor.

Sarah screamed, "Albert, do something!"

With nothing to fight with but his feet, Albert tried kicking Sammy away from unconscious, bleeding Clarence.

"Kick him hard!" Sarah yelled. "Don't let him get the gun!"

Hampered by the yards of duct tape still hugging his body, Sammy was having trouble moving fast.

Albert circled Sammy, and with one swift kick, knocked his legs out from under him.

"Kick him again!" yelled Sarah.

Albert lifted his foot...and the next thing he knew, he was flat on his back, next to the body of an unconscious Clarence, looking at the ceiling.

Holding Albert's foot in his one hand, Sammy cackled. "It takes more than yards of duct tape to get the best of me!"

"Sarah, be a dear," purred Sammy, as he removed the gun from Clarence's pocket. "Fill a plate for me."

Horrified, Sarah looked into the face of evil; Sammy was back in control.

"You heard what I said!" Sammy waved the gun. "Do it!"

Albert slowly pulled himself up from the floor. He couldn't meet Sarah's eyes.

Newly awakened, hungry Paul chose this moment to alert the world to his need.

"Not the kid again!"

Sarah shoved her plate at Sammy. "Here, take my plate. Eat, and I'll take care of Paul."

Between bites, Sammy motioned in the direction of the noise. "Keep that up, kid, and I'll take care of you permanently."

Permanently? Sarah was stunned. *Would he really kill Paul? But why wouldn't he? He probably intends to kill all of us.* "May I go pick him up?"

"First we get the rest of this tape off me." With a malevolent laugh, he added, "I want to thank whoever it was that did such a bad job of taping my hands."

Neither Sarah nor Albert moved.

Jamming the gun into Albert's ear, he roared, "Do it!"

With Paul crying in the background, the pair unwound the tape.

Sarah begged, "Please, may I pick him up now?"

"Not until we find the snowshoes." Waving the gun, he ordered, "You two first."

The trio stepped over Clarence's body and descended into the basement.

"Clarence said he knocked them over, so look on the floor."

"Found them," called Albert, "but I can't carry both of them with cuffed hands."

"So, Sarah, don't just stand there, go pick up the other one! Let's get this show on the road!"

"What show?" asked Sarah.

"That's for me to know and for you to wonder about," smirked Sammy. "Both of you…up the stairs, and no funny business."

As they neared the top of the steps, Sarah was surprised that she wasn't hearing Paul. Maybe he had cried himself back to sleep?

The three of them entered the room where Paul had been lying on the floor. The spot was empty.

Stunned, Sarah was speechless.

Keeping the gun aimed at them, Sammy backed into the kitchen to check on Clarence.

He wasn't there.

Sammy bellowed, "Clarence is gone and so is the kid! Give me those shoes!"

Fearing what Sammy would do to her baby when he caught up with them, Sarah frantically worked on the snowshoe's strap. The shoes were old, probably belonging to her Uncle Paul, the former owner of the house, and the strap was easily removed. Quickly kicking it under the sofa, she turned and handed the shoe to Sammy.

Perplexed, Sammy sat down and placed his foot on the shoe. "How do you attach the snowshoe?"

Albert pointed with his cuffed hands. "Look at the other snowshoe. It has a strap, and this one doesn't."

"Useless things," Sammy howled, and threw them across the room.

Trying to look innocent, Sarah asked, "Maybe the strap just fell off and is somewhere in the basement. Shouldn't we go look for it?"

"Oh, no you don't!" Sammy sputtered. "I see what you're doing! You want me to waste time looking for a strap instead of chasing after Clarence and your precious kid. Not gonna work! I'll catch him because I don't have the extra weight of carrying a baby who is crying his eyes out right now for his mama."

Sarah burst into tears.

"Isn't that tender, now?" mocked Sammy. "Enough of this. Up the stairs you go, and remember, I'm right behind you with a gun."

Sarah looked over at Albert who was shaking his head. "I'm sorry!" he mouthed.

Once again, Sarah found herself being pushed into what used to be the master bedroom, a room that she had refused to enter for years.

Sammy slammed the door behind him. The familiar grating sound of the turning key sent Sarah into hysterics.

There was nothing Albert could do to comfort her.

CHAPTER 22

IT WAS THE sound of voices that woke Lucky. He yawned, stretched, and then rooted around for Lady and the pups. He smelled something, but it wasn't a doggy smell. Then he remembered. Scrambling to his feet, he looked around, intending to exit the truck's bed the same way he had gotten on. Discovering that what had once been an open side wasn't open any more, he became restless. Pacing back and forth in the small area didn't help. Maybe the way out was jumping over the side. The distant voices were growing louder and closer.

Lucky settled down and waited. The doors of the cab opened and closed, a key was turned, and the truck moved.

WHEN THE MEN had headed into town for breakfast, they left behind a house full of disgruntled people; the party atmosphere was gone. What had started out five days ago as a light-hearted solution to a temporary energy failure had turned sour. The women weren't speaking to each other, and bodies that were used to soft beds were developing aches and pains from sleeping on the floor.

The phone rang. What a beautiful sound!

"Hello!"

"Hey, Clara, the power's back! Stick your head out the door and listen. The generator should have shut itself off."

The dogs, hearing the door open, raced past her. Joe was right; the generator was silent. As she waited for the dogs to finish their morning ritual and return to the house, she had the feeling that something was amiss. But now was not the time to figure out what it was; now was the time to get rid of all her houseguests and their animals.

Clara picked up the phone. "The generator isn't running! Oh, Joe, please tell me the outage is over!"

Joe laughed. "Honest to God, it's over for us. Some areas still don't have phone service, though. Go tell our squatters to vacate our property."

"With pleasure!"

It wasn't until the last guest had walked out the door and Clara was surveying her empty house that it hit her. Lucky hadn't been among the dogs that had gone past her when she was checking the generator. Was he ill?

With an anxious feeling, Clara ran into the area they had built for their dogs. Lady and Buddy were curled up, fast asleep.

Lucky wasn't there.

THE ROOM WAS freezing cold. Sarah and Albert huddled together as best they could, sharing body heat. Upon hearing the back door slam, they rushed to the window in time to see a bundled up Sammy attempting to fit his feet into Clarence's tracks on the unplowed driveway. The wet snow gave no resistance. With each step, Sammy sank into snow that was higher than his crotch. Based on the frequency of the times that he stopped to rest, pulling out a leg and stepping into the next track was tiring. Knowing that both people he had locked in the room would be watching him, he turned, and with a malevolent grin, waved his gun.

Sarah collapsed into a fetal position. Rocking her body, she keened, cried, and prayed; Sammy was going to kill her baby.

Helplessly, Albert watched his wife writhing on the floor. It should have been he and not Clarence who was risking everything to save Paul. He didn't even want to think about what Sammy would do to Clarence and the baby when he caught up with them. Sammy had the advantage; he wasn't carrying Paul, and he was using Clarence's foot holes in the snow.

Albert was about to leave his position by the window, when his eyes landed on the snow-covered vehicle that had brought Sammy to their home.

"Sarah, come here!"

"God, save my baby," sobbed Sarah. "Oh, Albert! What if he catches up with Clarence?"

"I have an idea!"

"My baby!" Sarah shrieked between labored breaths, "He's going to kill my baby!"

"Sarah, listen to me! Come to the window!"

"Oh, God, oh God!" she cried, rocking back and forth.

"Take a deep breath, and get yourself under control, Sarah! We've got to get out of this room!"

"My baby!" Sarah sobbed.

Reaching down, he took Sarah's hands and pulled her to the window. "See that pile of snow? Under that is the vehicle that Sammy drove here. As a prisoner, Sammy would have been chained in the back seat. Lord only knows how he got the key, but he did. Wanna bet that the key to our cuffs is in that van?"

"I want my baby!" Sarah howled.

Albert shook her. "Sarah, listen to me. Did you hear what I just said?"

"Oh, God!" Sarah pleaded. "Protect Paul."

Albert slapped her gently on the face. "We don't have time for this, Sarah! Pull yourself together!"

Surprised, Sarah quit crying.

"Tell me. When you were locked in here before, did you ever try to knock down the door?"

She swallowed a sob.

"We're wasting time! Talk to me! Did you try?"

"Did I try what?"

"Did you try to knock down the door?"

Sarah almost smiled when she raised her swollen eyes. "You really think I could have knocked down that door?"

"No, I don't, but at least now you're talking to me."

Sarah dried her eyes and sighed. "Even if I could have knocked it down, Sammy would have been waiting for me on the other side."

"If we're going to save Paul, we have to get out of this room. We're going to knock down the door....are you with me?"

She took a deep breath and squared her shoulders. "I'm with you."

"On the count of three...one, two, three!"

The two raced across the room, hit the door, and then collapsed onto the floor.

"Ouch."

"You can say that again!"

"Ouch."

"Listen!" whispered Sarah.

"You hear something?"

"Yes! The furnace just clicked on. The power must be back!"

Albert stood and hit the switch; the room filled with light.

"I'll bet the phones are working."

"If we can get to a phone, we can stop Sammy!"

With renewed hope, they hit the door with their feet, their bodies, and their cuffed hands.

"One more time!" urged Sarah. "Just pretend the door is Sammy, and hit it hard!"

"One, two, three!" counted Albert.

There was a resounding crack.

"A few more kicks ought to do it. Ready?"

With the shattered door behind them, they raced down the stairs to the telephone. Albert held a silent phone to his ear, and shook his head.

Breathing hard from the effort, Sarah puffed, "You find a shovel, and I'll get the broom. Even with cuffed hands, we should be able to get the doors open."

They draped a blanket over each other's shoulders, stepped into boots, and ventured outside. Long-legged Albert was shortening his stride, struggling to make a path for Sarah.

Side by side, the two of them hacked and whacked at the snow.

When Sarah was able to open the door on the driver's side, she gasped; the front seat was filled with snow.

"Albert, I don't believe there's a windshield. Come look at this!"

"Well, you come and look at this! There's all kinds of restraints in the back seat. I'll bet the key is here."

It was just a matter of minutes before Albert yelled, "I found it!"

Freeing Sarah's hand was the hardest; the rest was easy.

Albert headed for the house. Rubbing his raw wrists, a hot wave of hatred for the man who had cuffed him put urgency into his voice. "We need warm coats, boots, and the keys to the truck with the plow. It won't take us long to plow out to the main road. Hurry! With luck, we'll run into Sammy before he catches Clarence."

"But what if we do? Sammy has a gun and we don't."

"Then I'll run him over like the mad dog that he is!"

———————

RACING TO GET to the highway before Sammy caught up with them. Clarence could feel the sweat running down his back. Never had he walked though snow such as this. Had he done the right thing? He could only imagine how upset Sarah must be right now, but when Sammy threatened to do away with the baby, he didn't think twice before he thrust his feet into boots, grabbed any coat and hat that was handy, wrapped Paul in a heavy blanket, and ran out the door. The fact that it was Sarah's coat that he'd grabbed wouldn't have mattered if both his eyes hadn't been blackened, or his cut lip bleeding.

Those were the first things that the State Police noticed when Clarence flagged them down.

CHAPTER 23

THE TRUCK BARRELED south on I-75 with Lucky huddled in the back. Bothering him more than the physical discomfort of hunger and thirst was the sense that they were moving in the wrong direction. Struggling to his feet, he was checking the possibility of jumping over the side when the passing of an eighteen-wheeler truck changed his mind. His stomach growled. Following the men out the door this morning before eating breakfast was turning into a problem.

Although the sun's rays were growing a bit stronger as the truck traveled south, the ground was covered with a layer of new snow. Desperate to get off, he was once again entertaining the thought of jumping off the moving truck when it slowed down and pulled off the highway.

Taking a running start, Lucky jumped over the side of the truck's bed, landing in a snow bank. The two hundred pound dog was surprised when a sharp pain stopped him when he tried to stand.

The noise of running water was the only reason Lucky even tried to move. The rippling sound was pulling him toward the source. On three legs, he broke the ice on the approach to the shallow stream; the cold water felt good, and tasted even better. Finding a sheltered place, he stretched out, closed his eyes, and fell asleep.

"Hey you guys, look! A bear!"

"Dummy, that's not a bear, that's a dog!"

"You sure?"

"Yeah. Bears don't wear red collars."

Lucky opened his eyes in time to see boys running off into the woods. He knew about boys. After all, he lived with three of them.

As he watched them put their heads together, he wondered if they were thinking about a game to play. That's what his three boys did. He started to have bad feelings when all three walked out of the woods carrying sticks. Sensing danger, he tried to get to his feet; his injured leg buckled.

The boys approached the big dog cautiously, waving their sticks. They liked dogs, and they had no intention of hurting this one. They were just curious and a bit scared because of the animal's size.

One of the boys pointed. "Look! He has a red collar with white words on it!"

"I dare you to get close enough to read it."

"I'll do it," exclaimed the biggest one.

Lucky watched the boy edge closer. He looked a little like Jerry, so he didn't even growl as the boy turned his collar.

"It says, My name is Lucky."

"Cool!" one of the boys yelled. "That's my dog's name! I want that collar."

"You want it, you get it."

Feeling much more confident now that the big dog wasn't putting up a fuss, the boy removed the collar from around Lucky's neck.

The other two boys laughed.

"What's so funny?"

"How much does your dog weigh?"

"I don't know for sure, but I'd guess around thirty pounds. Why?"

"Look at the size of the collar! That would fit around your dog's neck at least three times."

The kid shrugged. "You're right," he said, and tossed the collar into the stream. "I can't use it."

Lucky watched it float away.

"Let's go home. It's dinner time."

AFTER FIVE DAYS of being closed, Molly walked back into her office, put the open sign on the door, and plugged in all the machines she had unplugged at the start of the storm. Just to reassure herself, she picked up the phone and listened to the beautiful sound of the dial tone. She had just put it back when it rang, startling her.

"Allen Real Estate."

"Molly, it's me, Clara."

Silence.

"Did you hear me?"

Silence.

"Oh, come on, girlfriend! Don't tell me you're still upset over the kitchen fracas!"

Molly sniffed. "Well, why shouldn't I be?"

"Because the whole thing was ridiculous!"

"Well, I guess maybe it was a little silly…."

"A little silly? Have you heard the men's version of our kitchen disagreement over the best way to load the dishwasher?"

"They wouldn't!"

"Yes, they would. I heard Joe talking to one of the other guys on the phone…it might have been Mitch. Joe was even imitating our voices."

"Well…."

"Molly, can we talk about something else?"

"Like what? And why aren't you here at your desk? Don't you have several closings to reschedule?"

"Lucky's missing again."

"Again? The last time he went missing, he came home with Lady and two pups. You think he's out starting another family?"

"I don't even know when or how he got out. No one seems to remember him going out the door. I'm trying to be calm this time. Last time, I really lost it, didn't I?"

"You were a basket case, Clara. You just have to believe that he's out there doing whatever it is that Lucky does, and keep remembering that he always comes back to you."

Clara wailed. "Molly, what will I do if he doesn't?"

"Get a grip on yourself, and get in here. You've got work to do."

CHAPTER 24

IT WAS MORNING by the time the three-legged dog made it to the outskirts of a small town. Hungry, thirsty, and hurting, Lucky was looking around every corner for relief from any one of his problems. A drink would be good, food would be better, and a nap would be the best of all. Walking past a building, his nose wriggled; he smelled something familiar.

He climbed the two steps with difficulty, and scratched on the door.

The lab technician tried to ignore the scratching sound coming from the entrance door to the veterinary clinic. Whoever it was that wanted to come in could knock like everyone else. The next scratch was accompanied by the sound of something bumping into the door. With an exaggerated sigh, she flung open the door. Looking up at her with pleading eyes was a huge black dog.

"Karen, what on earth!" exclaimed Dr. Hansen.

"Oh, good morning. Doctor."

"What do we have here?"

"I've no idea."

"Is he injured?"

"Looks like there's something wrong with his leg."

"Did someone just drop him off?"

"Could be. Too bad there's no collar."

"He's dirty. Bring me a bowl of water and some paper towels, and I'll clean him up a bit."

The dog eyed Karen as she placed the bowl of water on the floor. Dragging his body to it, he emptied the bowl.

"If he was that thirsty, he's probably hungry, too. Karen, do you have any food in your desk drawer?"

Karen shook her head. "Not a bite."

Dr. Hansen raised her eyebrows, "Not even a partially-eaten candy bar?"

Heavy-set Karen laughed. "When did I ever leave a candy bar partially eaten?"

"You got me there. I forgot who I was talking to," Dr. Hansen grinned.

After refilling the bowl with water, the vet gently cleaned the dog, who had gone to sleep. Other than the injured leg, the dog seemed in good shape.

"What are we going to do with him?" Karen asked.

"Wait a minute! What's with this 'we' thing! This is your problem!"

"Ah, come on, Dr. Hansen! Help me out here. What am I going to do with a dog so big it would take a crane to pick him up?"

"Well, he can stay here until his leg heals, but after that, you're on your own. The last thing that we need around here is another dog!"

"Shall I call the rescue team to come pick him up?"

"Yes. Tell them it will take about four of them to carry the dog to the x-ray room. I want to see how badly he's injured."

"While you're doing that, I'm going to look for a collar and a chain."

"Sounds like you're going to keep the dog."

"Oh, I'll put an ad in the paper tomorrow, but I just think he deserves a little bit of kindness today." Karen pondered, patting the big dog's head. "Wonder what made him scratch at our door?"

"His doggy sense told him there was a tenderhearted sucker waiting for him on the other side of it," Dr. Hansen teased.

"No, he just made a lucky pick."

"That would be a good name for him."

"What's that?"

"Lucky!"

"Lucky is what this dog is, so Lucky it will be. I'm sure I won't have him long enough for him to learn a new name. Somebody's probably out looking for him right now." She patted his head. "Wonder what his name really is."

"When he gets better, if no one claims him, you're going to have to take him home."

"That shouldn't be a problem. I'll just put him in my car and drive him home. Have you ever heard of a dog that doesn't like to ride in a car?"

"There's something else to think about. Are pets allowed in your condominium development?

"Yes, but I think there's a maximum size."

"Wanna bet Lucky is on the wrong side of that limit?"

"No bets here," grinned Karen. "Maybe I can hide him."

CHAPTER 25

CLARENCE WAS ALONE in the room. Through the walls, he could hear men's voices trying to sooth a crying baby. How had everything gone so wrong? The paper that the questioner had placed on the table in front of him was blank. He picked up the pen and twisted it, wondering what the printed words on the side of it said.

No matter how many times Clarence told his story, the police didn't believe it. How many times had he said they should call Officer Tom, and Tom would tell them about Sammy the Grunt? How many times had they asked for Officer Tom's last name, and who is Sammy the Grunt? Write it down, they'd said when they put him in the room. How could he write it down when he didn't know how to write?

Sammy had gotten close enough for Clarence to hear his cackling laugh and his taunts. It was the sound of a gunshot that preceded the description of what he was going to do to Paul that had put strength into Clarence's legs. His whole plan had been based on being able to flag down a passing car when he got to the main road. But what if the road hadn't been plowed open? There would be no passing car, and then it would be all over. In his anxiety, he'd lost his balance and fell.

Sammy was puffing, trying to close the gap between them. He'd wasted time yelling threats; it had been fun, but Clarence had gotten too close to the highway. Taking better aim, he'd pulled the trigger.

Lying in the snow, Clarence had sensed the bullet as it passed over him. The highway was so close! Was he going to make it this far, but lose anyway? Had he really thought that he was smart and strong enough to save his family from Sammy? Shielding the baby's body with his own, he'd prayed while he waited for the next bullet. The answer to his prayer, the distant sound of an approaching vehicle, was immediate. Challenging Sammy to shoot, he'd jumped up and ran to the middle of the plowed road.

Grinning, Sammy had taken aim at his easy target. Dumb Clarence! His grin had faltered when he saw that dumb Clarence was flagging down a State Police car.

Sammy wasn't grinning at all when he buried himself in a mound of drifted snow.

———————

STATE TROOPER FREED peered into the one-way window and studied the funny little fellow they had picked up on the peninsula. At first, they had thought that a woman was flagging them down; they'd heard the baby before they saw it. What was a man in a woman's coat, sporting two black eyes and a cut lip doing with a crying baby? His babblings had made no sense, and neither did his frantic story about being followed. There was no one there, and since there was only one set of tracks, the man had to be delusional.

If the phones had been working, Child and Family services would have been called to take Paul. Most areas had gotten back both power and phone service; the station had power back, and by afternoon, the phone company assured them that their service would be restored. Freed was aware that there was an Officer Tom Allen in the local police force. He was pretty sure that's whom the strange little man was referring to. As for Sammy the Grunt....was there really somebody by that name? He was hoping that the written account would make more sense than the man's story, but it didn't look as if the man was writing. According to him, the baby's parents might either be dead or locked in a bedroom.

The patrol car he had sent to the house on the vineyard had returned with the report that they had found the front door unlocked, but hadn't found any dead or locked up people.

CHAPTER 26

SAMMY CRAWLED OUT of the snowdrift, brushed off the snow, and shook his fist at the departing State Police car. Nothing seemed to be working in his favor. Clarence was going to spill his guts to the police, and that meant he had to disappear. He had the prison van, but both the van and the driveway were buried under several feet of heavy, wet snow. Could he hijack a car? He had two guns from the dead guards plus the one he had taken from Clarence.

His musings were interrupted by a scraping sound. Coming toward him down the driveway was a plow. Since Albert was securely locked in the bedroom, the truck was probably being driven by the man who Albert had hired to keep his driveway free of snow, but how had the driver gotten here? Sammy was puzzled, but with the plow getting closer, he didn't have time to figure it out. In his guard uniform, he looked like a solid citizen who needed help. With a good sob story about his car being stuck in the ditch, he'd get the truck to stop, throw the driver out at gunpoint, and get out of here ahead of the police.

With the nicest smile a man with smashed front teeth can have, Sammy waited for the approaching plow. Rehearsing his sob story in his head, he failed to notice that the truck was coming straight toward him.

Sarah was yelled at Albert who was losing precious minutes fitting chains around the truck's tires.

"We don't have time!" she shouted.

Albert didn't argue; he just did it.

She apologized later when the truck was able to move though the deep snow. Expecting to see either one of the men before they got to the highway, Sarah was getting anxious when no one appeared.

"I don't like this, Albert. There's no sign of either one....Sammy!" she screamed and pointed to a man who had appeared from behind a mound of snow.

Without a second thought, Albert turned the wheel, scooped Sammy up with the plow, and deposited him, along with a load of snow, by the side of the driveway. As they hightailed it down the plowed road, they didn't need to wonder if he'd survived; pinging bullets hitting the truck said it all.

Finally, breaking the silence, Sarah spoke. "So, what happened to Clarence and Paul?"

"We didn't see them with Sammy, so until we find out differently, let's pretend that they got away."

When Sarah bowed her head and closed her eyes, Albert patted her hand, "Don't cry, love."

"I'm not crying! I'm thinking up terrible things to do to that bastard Sammy! I wish we'd killed him with the plow!"

"Well, we didn't. He has all the guns, and the plow was the only weapon we had. We're almost to town. Our first stop is the police station."

There were shouts of relief when the phone rang for the first time in five days.

"Hey Tom, a guy from the State Police wants to talk to you," announced the officer who had grabbed the phone.

Tom picked up the phone and listened to the story about a strange little man they had picked up on the peninsula road. In the background, Tom could hear a baby crying.

"You say his name is Clarence? Could I talk to him?" Tom asked.

When Clarence grabbed the phone, Tom heard a voice that was punctured with sobs and hiccoughs. Trying to make sense out of what Clarence was babbling about Sammy the Grunt, baby Paul, Albert, and Sarah, he ordered, "Clarence, take a deep breath and slow down. Were Albert and Sarah all right when you took off with the baby?"

"They were down in the basement. Sammy took them down there to look for snowshoes."

"Did they want to go down there?"

"No. He has three guns. He made them go."

"And where were you?"

"On the kitchen floor. Sammy had hit me with the poker."

"Why did you run with the baby?"

"Sammy said he was going to silence Paul… permanently."

"Put the officer back on. I need to talk to him."

Tom looked up as two people rushed through the door. "Never mind. Albert and Sarah just walked in. Tell the officer we're on our way to his office."

Sarah jumped out of Tom's police van before it came to a complete stop. Tom had assured her that her baby was safe inside the state police station, but she couldn't relax until she had Paul in her arms.

Clarence's first reaction, when seeing Sarah approaching the station, was to hide. How angry was she going to be? Would she ever forgive him for running off with Paul? He was prepared for anything but the hug. Even before she grabbed the baby out of his arms, with tears streaming down her cheeks, she hugged him.

"Oh, Clarence! Thank you, thank you for saving Paul!" She kissed him on his cheek. "I'll take him now!"

The officers allowed Sarah the privacy of an interrogation room to change and feed Paul.

After hearing the story of life at the vineyard while being held by Sammy the Grunt, the police issued an all-points bulletin for the escaped prisoner.

Sarah shivered. "How can any one of us sleep, knowing he's out there?"

Tom had thought of taking them to his and Marie's house, but it just wasn't big enough. It wasn't as if these people were strangers. Both Marie and Sarah had babies, and they knew each other from the church's nursery. Every Sunday, they saw Clarence ushering and Albert playing the organ. Since Clara and Joe had a bigger house, he was going to call and ask them to take in the vineyard people. He knew Clara was home, elated over her newly emptied house, and here he was, about to fill it up again. He cleared his throat and said what he had to say. "You can't go back to the vineyard until we find Sammy."

"What are you talking about?"

"Sammy's still out there. Where is he going to go for shelter? You say he has three guns. Who's to say he won't show up at your house again? Until we capture him, no one is going to live at the vineyard."

Albert snorted. "That's easy to say, but not easy to do. Where would we go?"

Tom gave a silent prayer that Clara would go along with the idea. "I have to make a call before I can tell you."

Sarah frowned. "Are you sure? We do have a crying baby, you know."

"The woman of the house needs some distraction. Her dog has gone missing, and she spends most of her time either crying or out looking for him. It will be good for her to have something to take her mind off her lost dog."

"Are you talking about the dog that brought down Sammy in my vineyard?"

"That's the dog, yes."

"I laughed so hard at the picture in the paper. There was Sammy, who missed killing me by seconds, pinned to the ground by the big dog. I swear, that dog had a smile on his face!"

"That's our Lucky," grinned Tom. "He has done some pretty wild things in the past, but where he is now, nobody knows."

"Joe and Clara Skinner own that dog. You want us to go to their house?"

Tom reached for the phone. "If they'll have you."

FEELING DESPERATE ABOUT her missing dog, Clara was spending time in the new dog area of her house. Lady wasn't taking Lucky's absence very well, either. The usually laid-back dog had quit eating. Out of sorts, she searched the house, nipped at Buddy, and watched the door.

Clara picked up the pup, an exact replica of Lucky, and hugged him. "Where's your dad?" she whispered into Buddy's ear. Buddy's reply was a sloppy kiss. Clara sighed and put him down. She had tried to be strong, remembering the other times Lucky had disappeared; he'd always come home to her. Her posters, the ad in the paper, and the reward she was offering had produced nothing. It was as if Lucky had disappeared off the face of the earth. Remembering how she had fallen apart the last time he'd left home made her blush. This time she tried to keep it quiet; she cried when she was alone.

She was alone and crying when the phone rang. Taking a deep breath, she tried to remove the sound of tears from her voice when she answered.

"You want me to do what?" were her first harsh words to the question. "Come on, Tom! I just got rid of in-laws, out-laws, babies, dogs, and cats. Why me?"

"You aren't a complete stranger to them, Clara. They know you from the first encounter with Sammy in their vineyard, and you see them in church every Sunday. It shouldn't take us too long to find the escaped prisoner. Anyhow, Sarah needs a safe place to take care of her baby, and you need a little diversion from dog hunting. Lucky is going to come back when Lucky wants to come back."

Clara sighed. "My head knows that, but my heart doesn't."

"Can I take that as a yes?"

"Can you give me an hour? I have to change the linens on a couple of beds."

"You've got it. And thanks, Clara."

All Tom heard was a grunt before the line went dead.

CHAPTER 27

WHEN X-RAYS SHOWED there was nothing wrong that rest wouldn't cure, Karen talked Dr. Hansen into allowing the huge dog to stay in her office before she took him to her condo. Karen noticed that every time the door opened, he became alert…until he saw who had entered. Then he'd hang his head and tuck his tail tightly between his legs. Was he looking for someone to come for him? Karen tried to find the owner, but all her posters and ads in the newspaper went unanswered.

When he no longer limped, Dr. Hansen had reminded Karen of their agreement; Lucky's stay at the clinic was over. Dr. Hansen watched Karen and her new dog start their long walk home. Who ever heard of a dog that refused to ride in a car? The doctor was sure Karen hadn't walked so much in years. The two mile walk was easier on Lucky than it was on Karen.

The bed Karen made for him that first night was in the laundry room. Lucky watched her putting his water dish right beside his bed; he enjoyed the pat on the head as she bid him goodnight, but when she pulled the door closed behind her, he'd had enough. He howled.

"No, no, Lucky! The neighbors!"

When she opened the door, a black streak exploded out of the room, knocking her off her feet. Stopping just long enough to cover her face with kisses before stepping over her, Lucky raced into her bedroom, stretched out on the bedside rug, and closed his eyes.

Karen slowly picked herself up off the floor and wiped her face. Sighing, she crawled over the sleeping dog and into her bed.

Another problem reared its ugly head the next morning. Karen's plan to leave the dog alone in her condo was short lived. His howls were startling the neighbors long before her cab had arrived. On their long walk into work, she was beginning to have serious thoughts about her new dog.

Dr. Hansen really didn't like the idea of the dog roaming freely inside the clinic, but in the end, she was the one who supplied the big dog bed that ended up in the corner of Karen's office.

Karen was getting a lot of attention on their walks to and from work. In fact, a newspaper reporter followed her and Lucky to work and took their picture. Karen made sure that she and Lucky were standing in front of the clinic's sign. The phone rang a lot after the morning newspaper came out. People wanted to bring their animals to a clinic that was showing kindness to a stray.

It bothered Karen that Lucky was restless. Even when he slept, he was so aware of his surroundings that he immediately awakened at the least sound. She had expected to have problems with the expense of feeding such a big dog, but Lucky was barely eating.

His nose was cold, but his tail wasn't wagging.

CHAPTER 28

A NEW DAY WAS STARTING, and Karen wasn't feeling too good about it. Another morning meant another walk into work. The prediction for snow hadn't materialized; the pounding sound of rain hitting the roof didn't improve her mood.

It was pouring rain when they started their morning walk to work. She tried to share her umbrella with the dog, but by the time they reached the clinic, her shoes were full of water and Lucky was soaked.

Once inside, Karen unhooked Lucky's leash and made a face; the unpleasant smell of wet dog filled the room. Ignoring her attempts to rub him dry with a towel, he barreled past her to his dog bed in the corner, lay down, and closed his eyes.

If he had stayed awake, he'd have seen Karen sitting with her elbows on the desk, holding her head between her hands; she was rethinking the joys of dog ownership. Walking the dog back and forth to work was already getting old. She was wriggling her toes in her squashy, wet shoes when the door flew open and a man yelling for help and carrying a limp dog rushed in.

The noise woke Lucky. Looking around, he saw that not only was he alone, the door to the outside world was wide open. The most natural thing for a dog to do is to walk out an open door, and that's what Lucky did. The feeling that he didn't belong here had been growing, making him restless. He needed to be somewhere else. It was time to get back to what he'd left behind.

DRESSED IN A blue suit, white shirt, and red tie, Sammy drove carefully over the newly plowed road. The last thing he needed was attracting attention from anyone. He had no knowledge of what connections the almost naked dead man in the trunk had to the community. Hell, he could have been the town's mayor for all Sammy knew. He just happened to be the one who'd stopped to help when Sammy flagged him down. Not only was the man's wallet full of money, the gas gauge on the dashboard was registering full. If he weren't so hungry, he could be far away from this town before he'd need to stop. He tried to ignore the growing need for food from his grumbling stomach, but when a little diner's flashing sign caught his eye, he slowed down. What could be the harm of stopping there? It seemed as if the car had a mind of its own; the next thing Sammy knew he'd pulled into the parking area right beside the big eighteen-wheelers.

A harried-looking server was the only waitperson on duty and, having served him, didn't have time to give a second glance to him, the lone customer in the back booth, until he started to make strange sounds. Every head that turned to seek the source of the noise saw a nicely dressed man obviously in great distress; his hand was covering his mouth and his eyes were closed. The toothache that had initiated the appointment with the dentist so many days ago was back with a vengeance.

Pushing away the hot soup that had irritated the nerves of his smashed teeth, Sammy threw money on the table and ran out of the diner. With his mouth shut against the cold air, he breathed through his nose until reaching his car, starting the engine, and turning on the heater. Sammy had experienced pain in his life of crime, but no beating and no gunshot wound compared with aching teeth.

Driving erratically, Sammy headed out of town. Every breath of cold air sent a jolt of stabbing pain. With the car's heater set on high, the painful cold air began to warm up. Lifting his foot off the accelerator, he slowed down to the posted speed limit. Remembering how he had once gotten rid of several bodies, he started to look for a deep drop in the terrain that didn't have a lake at the bottom. In the past, it had been a boater on the lake who had discovered the body of the real estate agent he'd murdered. It was also the same drop that his car had gone over after hitting a deer. His tongue touched what was left of his beautiful smile after that accident.

A shock of pain made him renew his effort to find a dentist; getting rid of the body came second. The cold temperature would keep the corpse from smelling, so he didn't feel in a hurry. The dentist he would look for would be one with a small practice. There was no reason to expose himself to more people than was necessary.

Near the edge of town, he noticed a house set back off the road with a sign in the front yard. There it was, a ready-made solution to his problem. After the name of Dr. James Bloom were the initials D.D.S.

The long plowed driveway was free of cars. A light was shining out of the front window, evidence that the power had been restored. Sammy pulled into the driveway, and stopped directly beside the house.

DR. JAMES BLOOM, a retired dentist, looked out the window and watched a car pulling into his newly plowed driveway. An irritated frown puckered his brow. After five days of being held prisoner in his own house by three feet of snow, getting through the long to-do list would take him most of the day. The crucial item on the list was grocery shopping. After throwing out everything that had spoiled in the days with no power, his refrigerator and freezer were empty, and his pantry looked like Mother Hubbard's cupboard. Looking out the window, he could see that the man approaching his door was well dressed. Whoever it was, he'd get rid of him in a hurry.

Opening the door, Dr. Bloom stood with his arms crossed, ignoring the outstretched hand. "Something I can help you with?"

Sammy smiled, showing his broken front teeth. "I'm looking for Dr. Bloom, the dentist."

"I'm afraid I can't help you," Dr. Bloom said.

Sammy pointed to the sign. "You are Dr. Bloom, aren't you?"

"Yes, I am."

"So, why can't you help me?"

"I'm retired, and I suppose I should take down that sign, but the whole community knows that I no longer practice."

A hot bolt of pain reminded Sammy why he needed a dentist. "This is an emergency, Dr. Bloom! I have a terrible toothache!"

Pulling the door closed, Dr. Bloom replied, "I'm sorry about your toothache, but I suggest you find another dentist."

The smile on Sammy's face turned to a snarl. Inserting his foot into the opening, he stopped the door from closing. "I don't think so."

Dr. Bloom looked into the eyes of the man holding the door open and felt real fear. "Hold on now! I've already told you that I'm retired!"

"And I'm here to tell you, Dr. Bloom, that just for me, you're going to unretire."

"I really think you should…." Dr. Bloom's mouth snapped shut at the sight of the gun in Sammy's hand.

"For your own good, I suggest you take care of my problem. Turn around and go inside. I'm right behind you."

Dr. Bloom could feel his heart skipping beats. Sudden sharp pains that started in his chest and radiated down his left arm made him gasp for air. Feeling lightheaded, he reached out a hand and grasped the edge of the door.

"Come on, old man, move!"

Along with the feeling of doom, a sudden attack of nausea made him stagger.

Sammy scoffed. "If you're planning on pulling some stupid stunt right now, you can just for…."

Dr. Bloom lunged forward, opened his mouth, and spewed vomit all over the front of Sammy's suit.

The doctor was dead before he hit the floor.

CHAPTER 29

CLARA WATCHED THE closer from the title company explain to her buyers the content of the many pages they had to sign and initial. Closings were getting longer and longer with added documents and disclaimers. Since this house was in a farming community, there was a statement declaring that the buyers were aware that the house was situated in a rural district, and would accept the smells and noise of the farms in that area. The sellers disclosed that the house had passed the well, septic, and radon gas tests, no lead paint had been used in the house, Aunt Tillie had passed away in the guest bedroom, and they supplied a statement from a roofing company that had replaced the missing shingles that the house inspector, hired by the buyers, had discovered.

There are many details that have to be taken care of in the sale of a house, and Clara was good at details. Early in her career, she had missed an important one, and her embarrassment at being the cause of a stopped closing still rankled her. Since then, her work was done long before the closing.

With nothing to do but watch and trust that everything would go smoothly, her mind began to wander. Tom had taken the vineyard people to the mall. With diapers for the baby, a change of clothes for the adults, plus a few necessities, they had arrived at her doorstep; she'd been shocked at their condition. A hot shower was the first things they'd asked for. Five days and nights of never knowing what Sammy the Grunt was planning to do to them had taken its toll. Sarah was prone to weep without warning, and Albert, who had been unable to protect his family, exhibited hints of suppressed anger. She didn't know Clarence that well, but the man who'd always acted like a child seemed different. To save his family, he had taken charge of a dangerous situation, he'd defied Sammy, and he'd saved the baby. For Clarence, the ordeal had been a life-changing event. Clara noticed that he stood taller and looked her in the eye when he talked to her.

When she'd left her house, Albert was shoveling snow off the deck, Sarah was feeding Paul, and Clarence was playing with the puppy. Over soup and sandwiches, the stories they told of being held captive in a house with no heat, lights or water was truly hair-raising. Not knowing where Sammy the Grunt would next show up was a big concern.

The woman from the title company had to nudge Clara to get her attention. She was finished and the buyers and sellers were shaking hands. Clara smiled and pretended she'd been paying attention, said words of welcome to the new buyers, accepted her commission check from the closer, and headed for home. Maybe there would be a message on her answering machine about her missing dog.

———————

THE FIRST THING Karen noticed when she returned to her desk was the open door; the second thing she noticed was the empty dog bed. A glance at her watch told her she had been working with Dr. Hansen for the better part of an hour. How far could the big dog get in that length of time? Grabbing an umbrella, she ran out the door, hoping to catch up with him.

The tech from the x-ray department was disappointed when he didn't find Karen at her desk. He had just discovered that when they'd looked at the x-ray of the big dog's injured leg, they'd missed seeing an identification chip.

WHEN CLARA RETURNED home after the closing, the red light was blinking on her telephone; she had a message.

"I don't believe this!" she cried to Joe over the phone. "I just found out that my dog was found in the state of Ohio! Ohio? How in the world did he get to Ohio? And now they tell me he's disappeared again!"

"At least you know that he's alive! That's gotta count for something."

"Joe, did you know that Lucky had a chip?"

"Really? Oh, wait a minute. I'll bet if you'd call Dr. Phillip, you'd find out that he put it there after that episode with Syndee."

Clara was silent for a moment, remembering the Syndee incident. Lucky had been missing for days, and Clara was extremely upset. He had shown up at a veterinarian's office, carrying the little injured Syndee by the scruff of her neck.

When Clara' s silence lengthened, Joe became suspicious.

"Clara, please tell me you aren't thinking of driving to Ohio to look for your dog!"

"Why shouldn't I?"

"So you *were* thinking about it."

"Of course I'm going to Ohio! I had a long conversation with a woman named Karen. When he scratched at her door at a veterinarian clinic, he was limping. Joe, Lucky was hurt! They found the chip when they x-rayed his leg."

"Is the injury serious?"

"Not really. He just needed to be off it for a bit."

"So, that's what he's been doing? Recuperating?"

"He stayed at the clinic. The vet told Karen that she had two choices: get rid of the dog or take him home. I laughed when she described how she tried to get Lucky into her car."

"Now you're going to tell me that he howled when she left him to go to work, and they ended up walking back and forth...."

"That's the story. The eeriest part is that she named the dog Lucky. How strange is that?"

Joe sniffed. "Why wouldn't they know his name is Lucky? He wears a collar with his name on it."

"Not anymore. Lucky was missing his collar and tags when he showed up at her door. I've already called police departments and animal shelters in that area and given them a description. We can't count on every agency having a scanner to find his chip. And why can't I go to Ohio? I was told that these agencies keep a stray only seven days before they destroy it. How can I sleep knowing that?"

"Give the agencies a chance! A dog as big as Lucky is easy to spot. Please, just wait a few days before you do anything."

"A few days? Didn't you hear me say they keep strays only seven days before they do away with them?"

"Ohio is a big state, Clara."

"I know that, but I have to do something!"

"You have done something! You allowed Tom to talk you into letting the vineyard people stay at our house."

"Oh dear! I'd forgotten all about them."

"You invited them, and now you're going to leave?"

To Clara's credit, she realized she would be walking away from guests that she'd assured Tom were welcome. But wouldn't they understand?

"Sarah's a very capable woman. She loves Lucky...she *has* to love Lucky! After all, he saved her life. If he hadn't figured out that her handyman was Sammy the Grunt, we'd never have gone out there in the first place."

Joe knew when to give in. Clara would go to Ohio, and he would stay home with Lady, Buddy, and the vineyard people. This was not the first time in their relationship that Clara had placed her dog at the top of what was important in her life. Because he loved Lucky, too, Joe tried to understand. He just hoped Clara loved him as much as she loved her dog.

CHAPTER 30

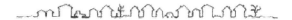

LUCKY FOUND THAT traveling at night had its advantages. For some reason, even though he was hoping for a pat on the head or a handout, most everyone he encountered shied away from him. He wasn't aware that it was his size that struck fear into the hearts of strangers.

Before they woke up and complained loudly, he had been managing to sneak a bite here and there from the bowls of tied up family pets. Water was easy to find if he followed its path.

The second morning since he'd walked away from the clinic found him at a small golf course. He found a sheltered snowless place near the clubhouse, paced around in a circle a few times, curled up, and went to sleep.

His slumber was interrupted several hours later by the arrival of a wedding party. Chattering people, clad in boots and warm winter coats, followed a shoveled path out of the clubhouse, heading for the snow-covered eighteenth hole. The bride, with her white gown hidden by a long coat, joined the bundled-up groom as they arranged themselves in the middle of those attending the ceremony.

Lucky sat up and watched with interest. What caught his attention was a little girl who was wandering away from the crowd. No one seemed to notice, not even the woman who had been holding the little girl's hand when they'd arrived. The wedding party blocked the sight of her walking toward a frozen-over pond.

He was the only one who saw her disappear when the thin ice on the spring-fed pond shattered.

CLARA HAD DRIVEN her car with the attached trailer down I-75 without stopping until she crossed the Ohio border. Stiff and sore from hours spent behind the wheel, she pulled into a rest stop, used the facilities, and then entered the restaurant.

She chose a table near the television set which was showing the local news. The sound wasn't on, but while waiting for her food, she entertained herself by trying to read the lips of the newscaster. The scene on the screen showed a wedding taking place on what looked like a snowy golf course. She watched as the camera took close-up shots of the couple gazing into each other's eyes, taking turns moving their lips; probably saying their vows. She was smiling at the happy scene when the camera quickly moved away from the couple to follow what looked like a running bear. The camera followed the animal as it jumped into a nearby pond. By now, the entire wedding group had abandoned the ceremony and was watching the animal. The camera left the pond scene and settled for a few seconds on a distraught woman before returning to the pond. The animal made its way to an object, grabbed it in its mouth, and headed for dry land. With waving arms, the wedding crowd was excitedly urging the animal on. Clara was wishing the sound were on; something interesting had stopped the wedding. It was when the bear-like creature surrendered a small child to the hysterical woman that Clara realized she was looking at her lost dog.

"Slow down, Clara! I can't understand a word you're saying."

Holding the phone in a death grip, she yelled, "Joe, I saw him, I saw him!"

"Ouch! Now, tell me again, a little slower, and not so loud, please!"

Clara took a noisy deep breath, cleared her throat, and started over. "I had just crossed the Ohio border when I stopped at one of those rest stop places. The television was on with no sound, but I got interested in a story about an outdoor wedding at a golf course...seems the bride and groom had met each other on the eighteenth hole. In the middle of the wedding, a young girl wandered away and fell through the ice on a frozen pond. No one noticed she was missing until an animal ran into the water and dragged her out. Joe, it was Lucky!"

"Oh, my goodness, Clara! Our dog did it again! Do you have him with you?"

"Unfortunately, no."

"No? Why not?"

"Because he's gone."

"Gone?"

"Yes. I immediately called the television channel and talked to the manager. He put me in touch with the photographer who was excited to talk to someone connected with the big dog, but since the wedding had taken place yesterday, he couldn't tell me anything about Lucky. By the time I went to the course and looked around, there was nothing there but a few dog tracks in a little hidden spot where he probably had slept. I also talked with people who had been at the wedding. It appears Lucky just vanished in the confusion that followed the rescue."

"Well, his sense of direction is good; he's heading this way."

"Joe, he has to cover the whole of lower Michigan to get home! How did he get into Ohio to begin with? Do you think someone kidnapped him?"

"Since he won't tell us, we probably will never know. Where are you?"

"I'm back in Michigan. I've called the police stations and animal shelters. Maybe some agency will pick him up."

Joe snorted. "Pick him up? With what?"

CHAPTER 31

FRESH FROM THE shower, Sammy stood in front of Dr. Bloom's closet and searched for something to wear. He was pleased to find a blue sweat suit that matched his eyes; the orange prison jumpsuit certainly hadn't! Life was good.

He hadn't been surprised that a dentist would have a supply of toothbrushes and boxes of small toothpaste tubes. Being careful of the sensitive front ones, he brushed teeth that hadn't been touched by a toothbrush in days. The vomit-covered clothes he'd stuffed into a plastic bag, and hurriedly tied it shut. Sammy had held his breath during the whole ordeal; the smell of vomit always triggered his own gag reflex.

Later, dressed in Dr. Bloom's winter coat and boots, he carried the doctor's body outside to join the one already in the trunk. Since there was no sense in courting interest in a strange car in the doctor's driveway, he moved the stolen vehicle to the back of the house.

His only problem was the lack of food. Five days of no power had spoiled everything in the refrigerator and freezer. The good doctor had already cleaned it out, and the only things in there now were condiments. The pantry did have several boxes of crackers, three packages of cookies, an unopened box of cereal, and a few cans of tuna and soup; he could survive a few days without having to leave the house.

By now, the vineyard people had told their stories to the authorities, and every agency in the state would be looking for him. The longer he could stay hidden in Dr. Bloom's house, the better.

Sammy had no idea why he kept looking into the refrigerator expecting to see something other than jars of mustard, olives, and pickles and an almost empty bottle of catsup. The cans of soup and tuna were gone. The last two days he had dined on crackers smeared with catsup. For last night's dinner, he'd found a candle to add to his dining pleasure. A catsup-smeared cracker with an olive balanced on top was his dinner, and a catsup-smeared cracker with a pickle on top was dessert. If he didn't want to starve to death, he had to go to the store.

In preparation for his venture into a world where every Tom, Dick, and Harry was looking for Sammy the Grunt, he had done a few things to his appearance. Since he hadn't shaved his face since the day he'd left the prison headed for the dentist, he had the start of a full beard. While rubbing his hand over his smooth, hairless shaved head, he realized his own mother wouldn't recognize him if she passed him on the street. That wouldn't happen because, as far as he knew, she was still in prison. A pair of the good doctor's sunglasses finished off his disguise. He couldn't drive the stolen car with the two bodies in the trunk, so that meant he would drive the doctor's car...and he would, if he could find the keys.

The keys were not to be found. Sammy searched the house from top to bottom, including every pant and coat pocket in the closet, under chairs, and especially between the sofa cushions.

The only place yet to be searched was the dead body in the trunk.

CHAPTER 32

DINNER WAS OVER. Joe and Albert sat with their elbows propped on the table, each nursing a cup of cold coffee.

"Hear anything from Clara?"

"Not since the wedding call."

"At least it sounds like he's heading in the right direction."

"Sounds like it."

Sarah was eavesdropping while she cleaned the kitchen. The stilted conversation the men were having was troubling to her. Joe was showing signs that he was getting weary of his visitors. Or could it be that he was showing resentment because Clara had left him with an arrangement that she had agreed to handle, and then had gone off to find her dog? Paul's crying at night wasn't helping, either. Joe was spending more nights at the fire station than he was spending at home. Feeling awkward around him, Albert tried to stay out of his way as much as he could.

The only person in the household who wasn't having any trouble with the arrangement was Clarence. He'd never lived in a foster home that had a dog, and therefore he was totally blind-sided by puppy love; Buddy had stolen his heart. Clarence walked, fed, brushed, and cuddled the pup that was looking more like his dad every day.

Buddy, who now responded to words like out, walk and treat, loved the walks that had Clarence on the other end of his chain. Walks that, at the beginning, were short, were now long and interesting. Parks and alleys had great smells, but nothing compared to the garbage can at the back of the butcher shop. Lady, on the other hand, was a lazy dog who turned up her nose at long walks. Clarence tried, but when she felt she had walked far enough, she just stretched out on the sidewalk. No amount of pulling on the chain changed her mind. It took the magic words, "Let's go home" to get her on her feet.

Clarence knew that Albert and Sarah, feeling uncomfortable living in someone else's house, were anxious for Sammy to be found so that they could go back to the vineyard. He himself was already dreading the day when he would be taken away from Buddy; first love is strong.

FIRE CHIEF Joe Skinner didn't look so good. Detective Mitch Hatch and Officer Tom Allen took stock of him over their plates of eggs, bacon, and pancakes. They had run into each other at the Omelet Shop.

"How's life at the Skinner Bed and Breakfast?" Tom asked with a straight face.

"Go ahead! Rub it in. I'd just gotten rid of all of you, and then Clara opens her big mouth and invites the vineyard people in UNTIL SAMMY IS FOUND."

Joe had yelled the last four words and people at close tables quit chewing and looked at them.

"Is it that bad?" Mitch looked puzzled. "You're at work most of the day, and by the looks of you, you're sleeping at the station."

Joe hung his head. "No, it really isn't that bad. Sarah's a good cook, she's keeping the house clean, Clarence is taking care of the two dogs, and Albert, for some reason, is staying away from me."

"So, what's the problem?"

"It's Clara. She's the one who invited the vineyard people to stay at our house, and then she left me with them while she's off looking for that dog of hers."

"Hmmm," Tom grinned. "Did I detect a little bit of jealousy in that last statement?"

"Come on, you guys, do you blame me?"

Tom and Mitch were silent.

"You aren't going to say anything?" Joe looked from one man to the other.

Mitch shrugged. "What do you think your life would be like right now if you hadn't agreed that she should go to Ohio?"

Tom laughed, agreeing with Mitch. "Admit it, Joe. You're better off with her in Ohio and not at home obsessing about her dog."

"She's not in Ohio anymore. Lucky seems to be heading north, so she's looking for him in southern Michigan."

"Getting back to Sammy, anything new on the guy?"

"Nothing. No one has reported seeing him, and believe me, there are many agencies looking for him."

Tom spoke up. "It sure has been quiet at the station. The only new thing in the past several days is a missing husband and father. Bruce Chamber's wife is pretty upset. She claims they have no financial or personal problems. In fact, they just had a baby last month, a boy."

"Another woman?" Mitch asked.

"She says no, but sometimes the wife is the last to know."

"Ah, he'll show up."

Joe looked at his watch. "Time to get back to work."

CHAPTER 33

WITH AN EMPTY feeling in the pit of his stomach, Clarence realized that the leash in his hand didn't have a dog at the other end; there was just an empty collar. Buddy, having escaped the collar, was already half a block away, running without restraints. With his heart in his mouth, Clarence watched the love of his life dodging walkers and cars. Buddy had made it through one intersection without getting hit, but another one was coming up.

Running as fast as his short legs would allow, Clarence was close to the next intersection when the green light turned yellow. He cringed when a speeding car, trying to make the light, swerved at the last second, missed the dog, but swiped a fire hydrant. The driver, an angry bald-headed man, got out of the car, screamed something at the pup, and then viciously kicked him to the curb.

Clarence took the time to shake his fist at the departing car before he picked up Buddy and hugged him.

SAMMY GLANCED IN his rearview mirror as he sped away from the intersection. He never should have gotten out of the car even though the damn dog deserved to be kicked.

If you didn't count the dog incident and the damaged car, the trip for groceries had been uneventful. No one had noticed that a stranger was driving Dr. Bloom's car. Very few things caused Sammy to question any of his actions, but when he opened the stolen wallet to pay for the groceries and looked at the picture of the man on the driver's license, shiver ran down his spine. His conscience didn't bother him most of the time, but sometimes a fleeting regret surfaced. Quickly, he pushed any condemning thought out of his mind. He was a survivor; if he had to remove objects along the way, so be it.

He had bought enough groceries to last for several weeks. If he could stay hidden long enough, maybe everyone would just forget about old Sammy the Grunt. The impossible thought made him smile; remembering that he had two bodies to get rid of erased the smile.

———————

MUTTERING TO HIMSELF, Clarence tightened the collar around Buddy's neck, and then made his way back to the fire chief's house. Buddy's narrow escape had scared him, but what the driver of the car had done infuriated him. If Clarence were an artist, he would have been able to draw the man's face; he remembered details. Another thing he remembered was the license plate.

Sarah met him at the door with a finger over her mouth. "Be quiet. Paul's sleeping."

"Man, what was his problem last night? I heard Joe get up around three-thirty and leave. Probably went to get some sleep at the fire station."

"No one got any sleep last night. Something's really bothering Paul, but his doctor says it's only colic, something she claims he'll outgrow."

"Before or after Joe kicks us out?"

Sarah shrugged. "If anyone has ever found a way to keep a baby from crying, I wish they'd tell me about it! I feel awful about keeping Joe awake at night. He's been in a terrible mood lately. Have you noticed?"

"It's hard not to notice. But it's Clara that's upsetting him, not Paul."

"Clara? How do you know that?"

"I overheard them talking on the phone. Joe wasn't holding back about how he feels. He wants her home."

"He's not the only one. Molly Hatch wants her back, too. Seem Molly is getting tired of taking care of Clara's buyers and sellers."

Clarence closed his eyes and pretended that it was Buddy who was lost. The feeling of sorrow that swept over him was so great he shuddered; he would be just as upset as Clara was. "I think Clara's right. If Buddy went missing, I'd do the same thing. Hmmm. Something smells good! What's for dinner?"

"Chicken and dumplings."

"Will Joe be here for dinner?"

"Why do you ask?"

"I know he's a fire chief, but could he help me find the driver of a car if I told him the license plate number?"

"Why, Clarence! What are you into now?"

Clarence told the story of what happened to Buddy when he'd slipped his head out of the collar.

"And the man yelled something at Buddy and then kicked him?"

"Yes, and he kicked him really hard, too. He could've broken his ribs."

"Joe wouldn't be the one to help you on that, but either Detective Mitch Hatch or Officer Tom Allen probably could. And you're sure you remember the numbers?"

"There are letters, too, and since Albert is teaching me to read, I know my letters now." He handed Sarah a piece of paper. "I wrote down what was on the license plate so I wouldn't forget it."

———————

CLARA WAS WORKING her way north on I-75, stopping along the way to connect with the police and animal control agencies. According to them, no one had reported seeing any dog that fit Lucky's description.

She was having morning coffee in her motel room in Rochester Hills when a short article in the local paper caught her eye. According to the Oakland Press, a woman jogger on the Paint Creek Trail reported to the police that a fellow jogger had made unwelcome advances. Her cry for help had brought a huge animal out of the woods. At first, she'd told them, she thought it was a bear that had chased the man away. When the police asked her to explain why she'd changed her mind about the bear, she answered, "Bears don't bark."

Clara visited the paper's office with a picture of Lucky. Her request for them to e-mail the scanned pictures to the jogger was granted, and a returned message from the woman confirmed what Clara already knew; it had been Lucky who had chased the man away.

———————

JIM KARNER LOOKED back over his shoulder, wondering why his wife wasn't behind him. Turning his bicycle around, he peddled back to see what had happened to Anita.

Paint Creek Trail runs through some heavily wooded areas that is heavily populated with deer. When he neared Anita and saw she was kneeling down, talking to something on the ground, his first thought was that she had found a fawn.

"Oh, Jim!" she called when he got nearer. "Look what I've found."

Jim propped his bike against a tree and walked over to see what she was talking about. Expecting to see a deer, he choked back a surprised yell and quickly took a step back. "Good Lord, woman! Is that a dog?"

"Of course it's a dog! I think he's lost."

Jim snorted. "How could anyone lose something that big?"

When Anita reached out a hand to show the dog that she meant no harm, he sat up, cocked his big head, looked her in the eye, and stuck out his paw.

"Oh, Jim, did you see that?"

"Yeah, I did. Now, come on. Let's finish the ride before it gets dark."

"Have you ever seen a dog this big?"

Jim snorted. "A dog that size would eat you out of house and home. Grab your bike, and let's get going."

"You're just going to ride away and forget about a dog that is probably lost and hungry?"

"Watch me."

"I don't think so."

Startled, Jim asked, "You aren't thinking about taking him home, are you?"

"It wouldn't be forever, Jim, just until we find his owner."

"Be sensible! We've just retired! Why do you want to be tied down with a dog?"

The dog, whose big head had been turning back and forth, following the conversation, got up and walked over to Jim. Sitting down, he cocked his head, looked him in the eye, and stuck out his paw.

The stern expression on Jim's face softened. The intensity of the dog's eyes, which were staring into his, was unnerving. Jim cradled the dog's big head in his hands. "Are you trying to tell us something?" he asked softly. In answer, Lucky placed a gentle kiss on Jim's cheek, flopped to the ground, and exposed his belly for Jim to scratch.

Anita laughed. "Has the dog changed your mind? Couldn't we take him home until we find his owner? Someone has to be looking for him, I just know it."

"Let's finish the ride, and if he's still here when we're ready to go home, I'll think about it."

With a pat on the dog's head, she retrieved her bike and followed Jim.

Lucky followed, too, but not close enough to be noticed. When the bikers retraced their ride to pass by the place where Anita had first noticed the dog, there was no dog to be seen.

After the ride, Lucky stayed in the background and watched Jim attach bicycles to a trailer that was hitched to their car. With Anita already in the car, Jim didn't see Lucky jump onto the trailer as he backed out of the parking space.

CHAPTER 34

JIM DROVE INTO his driveway and stopped to let Anita out before he pulled into the garage. Directly after her door slammed shut, Jim took his foot off the brake and pulled ahead. Anita's frantic yell stopped him.

Winding the window down, he stuck his head out. "Are you still upset because I wouldn't bring the dog home?"

"Well, if I were, I wouldn't be upset anymore."

"Are we talking in riddles now?"

"Just get out of the car, Jim. It's easier for you to see than for me to tell you about it."

With a disgusted-sounding sigh, Jim shifted the gear to park, got out, and walked to the back where Anita was pointing at the trailer. There, between two bikes, stood the dog. When he saw Jim, he sat down, cocked his head to the side, and offered his paw.

"Well, I'll be…." Jim was speechless.

"We didn't choose the dog, Jim, he chose us."

"And I suppose you're going to let that animal in our house? Lord only knows where he's been! He might even have fleas."

"Well, I suppose we could chain him outside until we give him a bath."

Lucky was watching the conversation, moving his eyes from mouth to mouth. When he recognized the hated word, he backed up a few steps.

"Did you see that?" laughed Jim. "He understood! Wonder what else he knows."

Anita paused while unlocking the house door, turned, and looked at the dog. "This is not a stray; this is a lost dog. I'll bet the owner is looking for him right nowwww...." Her sentence was interrupted by the dog that pushed past her and rushed into the house.

Jim followed Anita through the door. "Did you see where he went?"

"Toward our bedroom!"

The couple stood in the doorway of their bedroom and found the dog stretched out on the rug beside their bed. He heaved a huge sigh, and then closed his eyes.

"Well, I'll be!" whispered Anita.

Jim whispered back, "This reminds me of a joke. The question is, where does an elephant sleep?"

"Okay, I'll bite," Anita giggled. "Where does an elephant sleep?"

"Anywhere he wants!"

FIRE CHIEF JOE looked up from his plate of eggs and bacon and watched Detective Mitch Hatch and Officer Tom Allen making their way to his table.

"Good morning," he called. "Once again we meet at the Omelet Shop!"

"Do you eat any meals at home?" teased Mitch.

"Not many. It just doesn't seem like my house with Clara gone."

"So she's still on Lucky's trail?"

"She just keeps missing him. The last time he was seen was in Rochester Hills. Seems he chased off an unwelcome jogger."

Mitch cleared his throat. "I hate to mention this, but Molly is getting pretty tired doing Clara's business. Since Clara has a lot of buyers and sellers, Molly is working seven days a week."

Joe shook his head. "I love that dog, but I've about had it. I need Clara at home with me."

"We've mentioned this before, Joe. Clara would be miserable if she were at home with you when Lucky was out there, lost somewhere. You know that."

"Yes, I know that, but some nights, it doesn't help. I really miss her."

The three men sat quietly for a minute.

"Oh," Tom broke the silence. "The license plate number that you gave me? It belongs to Dr. Bloom, you know, the dentist who just retired."

"And the person who was driving the car wasn't Dr. Bloom?"

"Clarence gave a very vivid description of the man who almost hit Buddy, and it certainly wasn't a description of Dr. Bloom."

Joe shrugged. "Has anyone thought that it might be important to check on the old doctor?"

"For what reason?" Mitch wondered. "He might have loaned his car to someone. There's no law against that."

Tom looked thoughtful. "But would he have willing loaned his car to a man as vicious as the one Clarence described? What kind of a man would stop his car in the middle of traffic and get out just to kick a puppy? Dr. Bloom is elderly. Could someone be taking advantage of him? Maybe I'll think up a reason to drop by and check on him. Wouldn't hurt."

"Ever since braces, Dr. Bloom has been my dentist, so I was invited to his retirement party. I'm trying to remember a conversation he was having with another patient, something about going on a long vacation."

Tom nodded. "The retirement party was written up in the paper. The article said something about a vacation."

"Well, if he's on a vacation, then who was driving his car?" Mitch wondered.

CHAPTER 35

THE COFFEE HAD finished brewing, the bread in the toaster had popped up brown and crispy, the morning paper was on the table, and Sammy, still damp from the shower, was reveling in his newfound freedom. Any day that he wasn't behind bars was a good day.

With a cup of steaming coffee in his hand, he stood in front of the picture window enjoying the doctor's back yard. If the several birdfeeders meant anything, then Dr. Bloom had liked birds. While he watched, birds flew by the window several times, and then back to the feeder. Upon closer scrutiny, Sammy saw that the feeders were empty.

While he ate his breakfast, Sammy planned his morning. The first thing that he would do, he decided, was find where the doctor kept the supply of food and fill the empty birdfeeders.

Breakfast over, Sammy cleaned the kitchen, grabbed one of the doctor's coats and headed to the garage. He was so intent in his search that at first he didn't hear a vehicle pulling into the driveway; the slamming of a car's door got his attention.

Peeking out of the small window in the access door, Sammy's heart skipped a beat. There was a squad car in the driveway, and crawling out of it was the redheaded cop, the one he had stabbed at a Sunday open house. That, and a few other crimes, was the reason Sammy had ended up in prison.

From what he could see, there was something in the cop's hand. If it was a warrant granting permission to inspect the property, then

Sammy knew he had to disappear; the property would include the car he had hijacked that now had two bodies in the trunk.

Before he cleared his mind of everything that didn't have to do with his survival, he took the time to have a fleeting regret that he was about to leave behind several week's worth of food.

The garage contained Dr. Bloom's car and the yard and garden equipment. There was no second story, and the access door could be seen from the house. His only possible exit from the garage was a small window on the side away from the house.

Sammy spotted a sturdy-looking box, which he dragged directly under the window, stepped up on it, and tried to open the window. Many layers of paint had effectively sealed it shut; to get out, he'd have to break it. Would the redheaded cop hear the noise of glass shattering? If he were still in the house, maybe he wouldn't hear anything. Sammy didn't have a choice.

He smashed the window, stuck his head and body through, and then somersaulted to the ground. Recovering his breath, he scrambled to his feet and disappeared around the corner of the house, unseen by the redheaded cop.

With a "Congratulations on Your Retirement" card in his hand, Tom rang the bell several times; he pounded on the door, and when no one answered, he tried the doorknob. The door swung open. Tom stepped into a house that smelled of freshly brewed coffee. Someone was living here, so maybe the good doctor wasn't on vacation after all.

A quick search of the house produced an unmade bed, shaving equipment and a wet toothbrush in the bathroom, but no occupant. He was reaching for his cell phone to call the station when he heard the roar of his squad car's engine turning over. Running to the window, he saw his car, its wheels spinning and its brakes squealing, back out of the driveway and disappear. Tom frantically reached into his pocket, his heart in his mouth, afraid that he wouldn't find the key. When his hand grasped it, he breathed a sigh of relief; he hadn't left it in the car. Whoever had stolen his car had hotwired it.

———————

SAMMY'S HEART WAS pounding, his mouth was dry, and his hands shook. His feelings, fueled by the mixture of excitement, fear, and relief, were adding to the speed of the car. Taking deep breaths, he tried to regain control of his emotions, but hate for the redheaded cop kept interfering. If only he had paid more attention back when the kid had joined his gang, maybe he would have discovered that he had been a planted snitch. And then there was the annoying fact that the kid, really a cop, had refused to die when Sammy had stabbed him at a Sunday open house. Remembering brought a new hot wave of anger. The redheaded cop was the reason he was now driving a stolen police car while the safe warm house stocked with food was rapidly vanishing in his rear mirror.

Street smart, Sammy knew that he couldn't waste time thinking about revenge; self-preservation came first. He took another deep breath, arched his back, rolled his head, and assessed the situation. The first thing he had to do was ditch the police car. He had already realized that the wallet was back on the nightstand by his bed; he had no money. Noticing he was entering the business part of town, he reduced his speed and watched for any opportunity. A woman pulling into a parking space caught his eye. He braked and watched as a man in a white coat stepped out of the drugstore with a package in his hand. The woman driver, without shutting off the car's engine, stepped out and met the man on the sidewalk. The woman smiled as the man handed her the package. The smile vanished when she turned and saw her car pulling out of the parking space and driving away.

Tom's wife, Marie, screamed. Baby Logan was in the backseat of the car.

SAMMY DIDN'T DARE look in his rearview mirror as he sped off in the hijacked car. Putting distance between him and the screaming woman before the police got into the act was imperative. Just the thought of an impending chase made him feel alive. Twisting and turning to throw off pursuers, he slowed down, took a deep breath, and reviewed his options.

Once again, just as it was when he'd escaped during the snowstorm, he had been thrown into a situation without an action plan. Grinning to himself, he reveled in the thought that he hadn't lost the knack of sensing an opportunity. How had he known to stop and watch the woman who was pulling into a parking spot? Man, he was good! Remembering the police car he'd left with the engine running and the driver's door wide open, turned his grin into a chuckle. Wouldn't the redheaded cop be in hot water for letting his police car be stolen? His chuckle ended when he remembered all the trouble the little snitch had caused. Being reprimanded for being careless with the cop car was not nearly enough. The next time he had a chance, he'd make sure the snitch was paid back for everything.

No doubt, the lady was still screaming bloody murder, and it would take some time before the search for her car got serious. He figured he could safely put a few minutes behind him before he started to look for a replacement. Malls are always a good place to switch cars, so that's where he headed. If he were lucky, he'd pick the vehicle of a worker who wouldn't be looking for it until the end of the workday.

The parking lot was full. In the back of the lot by the huge mounds of plowed snow, he spotted a car that had an empty space beside it. He pulled into the space and parked. Glancing around, he saw that he was alone. The conveniently unlocked faded brown car he intended to hotwire was a nondescript older model.

It was just something he always did before stealing a car...he looked under the floor mat. There was the key, bright and shining, just begging for him to pick it up and use it. So he did.

Sammy drove the older vehicle out of the parking lot, leaving behind Marie's car with Logan asleep in the back seat.

Marie's screaming brought people out of the stores. While concerned spectators huddled around her, trying to understand what she was screaming about, someone called 911. It took a shot administered by the emergency crew to calm her down before they could transport her to the hospital.

By that time, Sammy had made it to the mall and had switched cars. The description of Marie's car had gone out, and all agencies were checking similar cars that were heading out of town.

THE FRECKLES ON Tom's white face matched his tousled red hair. As he paced the hall that ran past Marie's hospital room, the depth of his despair was frightening. He blamed himself. If only he'd locked the police car! If only....

Tom's cell phone vibrated in his pocket. Because the use of cell phones was prohibited in this part of the hospital, his first inclination was to ignore it. A quick glance at the origination of the call changed his mind. Rushing to an area where cells were allowed, he answered, "Officer Allen here. What did you find?"

"Lots of fingerprints and two dead bodies in the trunk of Bruce Chamber's car!"

Tom sucked in a breath. "Two? One of them Bruce?"

"Yes."

"So it wasn't another woman," Tom muttered. "His poor wife. They just had a baby last month."

"That sucks."

"Who was the other one?"

"The retired dentist."

"And the fingerprints from the house?" Tom closed his eyes and said a prayer. *Please, please, God. Don't let the answer be Sammy the Grunt.*

"The prints in the house belong to a man called Sammy the Grunt. Ever hear of him?"

A subdued Tom returned to the hall outside Marie's room. There was no way that he was going to tell Marie who it was that had driven away with Logan. They both knew that Sammy hated Tom. The thought that this evil man now had Logan was terrifying.

He ran his hands through his red hair and shook his head. Now he knew that he could quit obsessing over not locking his police car. A locked car door wouldn't have stopped a career criminal like Sammy. Logan, his son, was gone. Sammy had driven away with the most precious thing in Tom's world.

Becoming a father had brought surprises. Never had Tom entertained the idea that he could have such an intense love for a child, his child. He'd give his own life for his son, of that he had no doubt.

While he paced, Tom had moments, sometimes several seconds long, when he'd forget that Logan was gone. Then reality would hit, and the pain that followed was sharp and deep.

Marie was in bad shape. The knowledge that she had left Logan in an unlocked car with the engine running, even if it was just for one minute, had devastated her. Marie, a nurse at this hospital, was one of their own. Both doctors and nurses kept peeking into her room, checking on her.

CHAPTER 36

CLARA DROVE OUT of Rochester Hills and headed north toward home. Her heart was heavy for several reasons. Not finding her dog was the one that hurt the most right now. It was time to go home and pretend that even though she was sad, life was going to go on just fine without Lucky. The only time she would cry would be when she was alone. She could do it.

The problem with Joe was serious. Lately, when she talked with him on the phone, the loving tone was gone from his voice. True, she had left him with the vineyard people to take care of, but he loved Lucky, didn't he? Why was he so upset over the few days she had taken to find her dog?

Even though Molly had let her know, in no uncertain terms, that she was tired of taking care of Clara's buyers and sellers, she wasn't too worried. She could appreciate how hard Molly was working, because she had kept Molly's real estate office open for months before and after Molly's twins were born. And then there was the fact that she, Clara, had won several Realtor of the Year awards….

As much as she hated to give up her search, she felt she had no choice. There were too many problems; it was time to go home.

When her cell phone vibrated, she put on her turn signal and pulled off the road. Maybe someone was calling about Lucky. Maybe someone was calling to say they had him and would keep him until she showed up. Maybe someone was calling to…

"Hello?"

"Clara, it's Tom."

"Hi, Tom! Are you calling me because Joe asked you to? He's getting pretty fed up with me, isn't he?"

"No, Joe didn't ask me to call. I just thought you'd want to know...."

"Tom, are you crying? Has something happened to my sister?"

What Tom told her was unthinkable. Long after the conversation was finished, Clara had sat holding the silent phone. Her poor sister. Knowing Marie, Clara was sure she'd smother herself with shame and guilt. Marie was the type of person who was quick to forgive the mistakes made by others, but not her own. In a case such as this, she would be her own worst enemy.

Marie needed her. Bowing her head, she said a prayer for her lost nephew and her lost dog, pulled back into traffic, and headed north.

"COME, BAILEY, TIME for your dinner!" Anita yelled out the open kitchen window. She could see the big dog lying in her neighbor's much-prized landscaped yard, while the resident yappy poodle crawled all over him.

"Oh, Jim, go and get Bailey before Lilly sees him! The Winter Garden Club is scheduled to visit her yard tomorrow!"

Jim stepped out of the house and called, "Bailey, dinner!"

Lucky's ears twitched. He had no idea about the first word, but he sure knew what *dinner* meant. His struggle to get on his feet sent the poodle flying off his back. Ambling toward Jim, he left behind a large patch of freshly dug holes and a limping poodle.

Jim shook his head. Since Bailey seldom wandered from their yard, they had been allowing him to run free, off the chain. However, things had changed when Lilly lost her heart to a homeless poodle -- the Humane Society's featured Pet-of-the-Week. For Lilly, it was love at first sight, and unfortunately for her lawn, the poodle had the same effect on Bailey. There had been a few harsh words spoken, and then the declaration: Bailey was not welcome in Lilly's yard.

Jim saw a big problem rearing its head. They had found early in their relationship with the dog that he howled when he was tied up. Jim was pretty sure Lilly wouldn't like the howling, either. Dog ownership had its drawbacks.

That thought reminded Jim of another drawback. What were they going to do with the big dog when he and Anita made the trip north for the twenty-seven mile Ice Man Cometh bike race? He had signed up for that race months ago. The yearly race that starts in Kalkaska and ends in Traverse City is scheduled during Michigan's cold season. Anita had always made the trip with him when he'd ridden the race before. It was her chance to visit with good friends who had built a house on a quiet little lake when they retired to Traverse City.

What were they going to do, now that they were owners of a huge dog? Would Anita have to stay home? He'd warned Anita that this was going to happen, but he'd known from the many years he'd been married to her, that when she set her mind on something, she usually got her way.

Lucky looked around after he'd thoroughly licked the now empty bowl, hoping someone was there to see him do his sad-eyed plea for more food. Since no one was there to impress, he did a doggy shrug and headed for the door. They might not be around to see him beg, but they always seemed to come running when he scratched on the door.

"Bailey, stop that!" Anita growled. Opening the door, she followed the dog outside. Before he had a chance to think about where he wanted to go now that he was out of the house, she had him hooked to the chain.

"Now, behave yourself, Bailey. No howling!" she ordered.

Without even a pat on his head, Anita went back inside. Lucky didn't hesitate. He pulled on the hated chain until it broke, leaving behind a short section of it still attached to his collar. Lately, the feeling that he needed to be somewhere else had grown stronger.

Without a backward glance, Lucky walked away.

CHAPTER 37

THE TEMPERATURE HAD fallen; more snow was predicted. In the back of the mall's parking lot, the cleanup of last week's snowstorm had left mounds of snow fifteen feet high. There was only one car parked near them, and it wasn't hers. Had she forgotten where she'd parked this morning? The tired-looking woman shook her head in despair. What else could go wrong with this day? Her legs hurt from the eight hours she had stood on them, working behind a counter for minimum wages. Thank God, she'd been talked into buying a cell phone, because walking back into the mall to find a security guard wasn't even a possibility. Fumbling in her pocketbook, she found the phone and dialed 911.

The police arrived shortly, took the woman's description of her stolen car, and since she had no one to call, agreed to drive her home. As they were getting into the police car, the woman pointed at the lone car that remained in the back of the lot. "Oh, by the way, I heard some strange sounds coming from that car."

"What kind of sounds? Maybe a dog?"

"More like a cat."

The police officer, an avid cat hater, hesitated but a moment before he started the car and drove away.

SAMMY WAS PLEASED. He wasn't being followed, and until the owner figured out his car had been stolen, he was safe. His foot eased off the gas pedal; now was not the time to call attention to himself. Although the car was old, someone had taken good care of it, and he congratulated himself for stealing a car that could get him out of the area.

A nagging little voice in his head reminded him that he had no place to go; he was a wanted man. Probably his picture was posted all over the area. Reaching up to rub his shaved head, he felt a bit of relief knowing that he no longer looked like the man in the picture.

Where could he hide until he could come up with a plan? A glance in his rearview mirror showed nothing but an empty road behind. Most likely, the owner of the car hadn't yet discovered it was missing. So far, so good.

With no destination in mind, Sammy drove on, hoping to put miles between him and the town. Feeling the need to listen to something other than humming tires, his eyes searched the dashboard for the radio knob. His feeling of elation ended when he noticed the gas gage. Empty. Had he stole a car that had an empty gas tank? As if it were waiting for Sammy to acknowledge the situation, the engine started to cough and sputter, then died in the middle of nowhere. Closing his eyes, he pictured the wallet on the nightstand, wishing he could reach out his hand and grab it.

The next best thing would be for some Good Samaritan to come along. As if on command, a car appeared in the distance with its turn signal flashing. He was about to climb out of his disabled car and meet his rescuer when he saw the lights on top of the vehicle; it was a police car.

Sammy ducked low, crawled over to the passenger side of the car, opened the door, and slid out. There were weeds in the ditch, and Sammy was grateful for that. Crawling on his belly, he managed to reach a treed area by the time the police car had stopped.

Holding his breath and afraid to raise his head to look, he could hear the cop talking on his cell phone, relaying the message that he'd found the reported stolen car. Goosebumps spread up and down his arms when he chanced a peek through the weeds and watched as the cop shielded his eyes to search the very area where he was hiding. He didn't breathe easily until the cop crawled into his car and drove away.

The small patch of trees ended at the mouth of a street…the row of houses that backed up to the woods had well-kept lawns, basketball hoops above garage doors, and dogs. Lots of dogs. He could hear them barking at the intrusion of an unknown. Ever since he'd had his run-in with that huge dog in the vineyard, he'd hated dogs.

MARY, A STREET PERSON, pulled her many layers of clothes tightly around her shivering body. Where was she going to spend the night now that she'd been kicked out of the shelter? *They'll be sorry tomorrow when they find my dead frozen body*, she thought. *They'll cry at my funeral and ask my forgiveness, but I'll show them! I'm not forgiving any of them, especially not that bitch Selma who stole my special seat at the table. I hope her nose is still bleeding!*

The snow was coming down soft and fluffy. Sticking out her tongue, she caught a flake, which reminded her that she'd missed dinner. Since leaving the shelter, she had been walking aimlessly, too angry to pay attention to where she was going. Looking around to get her bearings, she realized that her walk had taken her in the direction of the mall. That made her think about some of the thrown-away food she sometimes found in the trash behind a restaurant there, so she continued in that direction

Reaching the back of the mall, she stood for a moment looking up at the fifteen-foot mounds of snow that the plows had scraped from the parking lot. The awful five days when the storm had knocked out the power had been a bad time for the homeless. She had lost several friends that week.

About to continue her journey to the back of the restaurant, the sound of a crying baby cut into her soul. No, no, no! She shook her head, trying to stop the bad memories filling her brain. It was all in her head. How many psychiatrists did it take to convince her that there was no crying baby? She had to quit hearing it or they'd send her away again. Turning her back on the car, she tried to walk on, but the baby's cry was just too real.

Would it really be a bad thing if she just checked? Who would know? Slowly she approached the car, brushed the snow off a window, and looked in. What she saw made her breath catch in her throat. Back before the bad time, she had owned a bright red convertible, so she knew that the shiny thing dangling from the ignition was the key. The thought of spending the cold and snowy night in a warm car was almost too much to hope for. With a shaky hand, Mary opened the door. It was hard to ignore the baby's cry because now it was really loud, louder than even in the worst of her bad dreams. She crawled in, turned the key, and held her breath until the heater blew delicious warm air into the frigid car. Mary smiled. Now if she could turn off her head and shut out the crying, life would be good.

Hours later when the night security guard investigated the parked car with an exhaust plume visible in the cold air, Mary was sound asleep with her head on the steering wheel, and Logan had cried himself into exhaustion.

———————

MARIE DIDN'T WANT to wake up. Sleep was her only relief from the crushing and devastating remorse she was feeling for leaving

Logan alone in the car. She was the reason her baby was out there somewhere, hungry, alone, and probably cold. Was he even alive? Oh, he had to be alive!

Please, God," she prayed. *"Let him be alive! Please don't let my stupid mistake cost him his life!*

Marie had another thing to feel guilty about. She'd caught a cold from one of her patients, taken it home, and shared it with Logan; her baby had his first cold because of her. Logan's pediatrician had called the drugstore pharmacy with a prescription for him. Not being able to breathe through a stuffed nose had kept the baby awake most of the night, and when he had finally fallen asleep in the backseat of the car on the way to the drugstore, Marie hadn't had the heart to wake him. She was picking up two prescriptions; one for her, and one for Logan. Talking the pharmacist into meeting her outside the store with filled prescriptions for both of them had seemed like such a good idea. How wrong that had been!

Maybe someone kidnapped Logan because they wanted a baby? Mentally, she shook her head. No, she had overheard conversations she was not supposed to hear; the word was that Sammy the Grunt had hijacked her car. What would that evil man do when he discovered he'd stolen a car with a baby in it? She didn't want to think about that, either.

The sound of footsteps in the hall made her cringe. Since she had worked in this hospital for years, the doctors and nurses knew her. Of course, they were concerned, but she didn't need any more sad faces and sympathetic words. She braced herself, put on a fake smile, and waited for the door to open. She could do it one more time.

The door seemed to take forever to open. Marie's face muscles were quivering from holding the fake smile.

Framed in the open doorway, Tom paused long enough to gaze at his wife with loving eyes. He'd fallen in love with this woman before he even knew her name. The remorse she was feeling for leaving Logan alone in the car had put her in her own private hell. He was about to release her from that hell.

He crossed the room and laid Logan in her outstretched arms.

Confused by all the fuss being made over her, the street person named Mary closed her eyes. If she couldn't see them, maybe they couldn't see her. What had she done to cause all this commotion? She had crawled into a stranger's car and spent the night. Shouldn't she be punished for doing something like that? She had been careful not to mention that she'd heard a baby crying. That was a no-no. Saying that would get her sent away again.

Oh, oh. Mary stiffened her body when she saw a tall woman with her arms wide open heading her way. Swinging the small woman off her feet, the woman sobbed. "Oh thank you, thank you! You saved my baby!"

Mary blinked. "Then there really was a baby?"

Marie stepped back and held Mary at arm's length. "Of course there was a baby. Didn't you hear him crying?"

A blank look spread over the woman's face. In a trance-like state, she chanted: "My name is Mary and there is no crying baby my name is Mary and there is no crying baby my name is Mary and there is no...."

A puzzled Marie watched as an attendant gently put her arm around Mary and led her away. "Come with me, Mary. I have some nice hot soup for you."

———————

LOGAN'S STAY IN the hospital had been a short one. Along with congestion from his cold, he was found to be dehydrated and hungry, but Mary had supplied the miracle that had kept him warm. Several doctors and many nurses hovered over him, checking to make sure he'd survived the ordeal. Now, clean, fed, and warm, he was pronounced well enough to be taken home.

Marie wasn't looking forward to visiting the police station with Tom to retrieve her stolen car. Did she ever want to get into that car again? Would she ever be able to rid herself of the sight of seeing that car pulling away from the curb, taking Logan from her?

Tom felt her shudder and pulled her into a tight embrace. Holding her close, he wondered if she would fully recover from the experience of losing her child. He knew the history behind Mary, the woman who lived on the street. She had once been a happy woman who, unfortunately, had rolled over in bed and suffocated her baby. Having a loving and supportive husband hadn't been enough to keep Mary sane. After years of sticking with her while she worked through one psychiatrist after another, he finally gave up when she rejected him and took to the streets.

Tom had felt Marie pulling away from him during the ordeal. Losing Marie in the future scared him almost as much as losing Logan today.

CHAPTER 38

LUCKY STRETCHED OUT in the soft dirt from the good-sized hole he'd dug in the prize-winning landscaped yard. It felt good to be back, close to the place where the two nice people lived. He still had a nagging feeling that he needed to be somewhere else, but right now he was hungry and his leg hurt.

His eyes grew heavy waiting for morning when he knew someone would come out to pick up something off the porch. Whatever it was, the people looked at it while they drank vile smelling stuff. The stink used to make his sensitive nose hurt, but over the years he had gotten used to it. Anyhow, he put up with the stench because after they quit looking at the thing that had been picked up on the porch, there was a good chance that someone would take him for a walk.

Lulled to sleep by the quiet night, Lucky's feet moved. In his dream, he was running toward someone who was anxiously calling his name.

"Anita, we should have been on the road an hour ago! What's taking you so long?"

"Just hold your horses, Jim! If you're in that much of a hurry, you should have helped me clear away the breakfast dishes. Forty years of marriage, and you still aren't trained!"

"Need I remind you, woman, that you train dogs, not husbands?" Jim chuckled.

"Speaking of dogs, I'm still having trouble over the Bailey mystery. Don't you wonder what got into him all of a sudden? He broke the chain and just took off…to go where?"

"Didn't you ever wonder why he was in the park in the first place? Maybe we were just a resting station on his journey to somewhere."

"Jim, you've been reading too many dog books. The tale of a dog's instinct helping him find his way back home makes a good story, but I wonder if it ever really happens."

"Sure it does."

Anita rolled her eyes.

Jim ignored her. "Anyhow, the bike's already on the trailer, so I'm ready to go when you are. When did you tell the Barkers to expect us?"

"I'll call them on my cell phone once we actually get into the car. It will be good to see our old friends again."

Jim poked Anita in the ribs. "Be honest now. Since there's usually a pitcher of margaritas at some point in the visit, are you sure it's the Barkers you're eager to see?"

"Ah, go on, Jim! We shared it with you last visit."

"I remember it fondly! Now, is your bag ready to be put into the trunk?"

"Mine's ready, but is yours? Are you sure you have all your biking clothes packed? Remember, it's cold in northern Michigan this time of year."

"Yes, woman, I remember. According to the weather report, it's snowing up there. That will make the twenty-seven miles through the woods pretty tricky."

"You men!" Anita shook her head.

Grabbing two overnight bags, Jim headed for the door. "Meet you at the car!"

Lucky's dream was cut short by the sound of voices. Opening his eyes, he saw a car with the trailer attached about to pull out of the driveway. Leaving behind a big circle of freshly dug dirt, Lucky ran and jumped onto the moving trailer.

CLARA THREW BACK her head in an unsuccessful stab at a high note. The trip back home seemed to be taking a lot longer than the trip down to Ohio. Maybe that was because she wasn't looking forward to seeing Joe and his scolding eyes. Maybe if she'd found the dog, Joe would be so relieved that he'd forget that he was angry with her. Maybe….

Not wanting to dwell on the inevitable, she turned up the volume on the radio and resumed singing. What was it about her singing that made people stare at her in church? And last Sunday, it had hurt when the man sitting next to her leaned over and whispered, "Gee, I didn't know you couldn't sing."

She just wouldn't let herself remember the painful episode when she'd visited an all-female a cappella singing group with the idea of joining them. Because it had been advertised as a visiting night, two other hopeful singers had shown up. The audition was easy, and she was sure she had passed. Come on! How could you not sing "Happy Birthday"? The three of them sang it high, and the three of them sang it low. They sang the scales high, and then they sang the scales low. Later in the evening, Clara had a chance to sneak a peek at what the director had written. After one name, she had written: Good range. Has lots of singing history. Baritone? After the other name, she had written: Yea! A bass! Seems eager to sing with us. After her name, there was just one word: loud. She was puzzled when they hadn't invited her back.

Ending a song with what she was sure was a harmony note, she was pleased to see the exit for West Branch coming up. There were many chain restaurants at this stop, and since she was hungry, this was a good place to grab something to eat.

"ANITA, WAKE UP!" Jim poked his sleeping wife. "Some company you are!"

"Wh…wh…what?" muttered Anita. "Are we there yet?"

"No, we're not there yet, but we're coming up to the West Branch exit. You always like to stop here."

Anita stretched. "A cup of coffee would be good right now."

"Just coffee? Aren't you hungry? I am."

"So what's new about that? You're always hungry! Oh, I guess I could handle a sandwich."

Jim swung into the exit lane. "Any place in particular? There are a lot of them to choose from."

"Just pick one, Jim. A sandwich is a sandwich, no matter where."

"Okay. How's this one?" he asked as he pulled into one and parked beside a car with a trailer attached to it.

"Would you look at that," Anita marveled. "A miniature fire truck! Wonder who rides on that trailer."

Jim snickered. "A tiny little fireman? Come on, I'm starving!"

With a sigh of relief, Lucky relaxed. The bike trailer he'd chosen to ride on didn't have safety straps to hold him when the car made unexpected turns and stops. There were claw marks that stopped at the very edge, marking his struggle to remain on the trailer. He stood and stretched out muscles that he had held tense for so long.

Lifting his nose into the air, he sniffed. What was that smell? The aroma that was coming from a very familiar vehicle was making his heart beat fast; it was the smell of home. Without a second thought, he jumped off the bike trailer, ran over to the next trailer, and jumped on.

CHAPTER 39

CLARA PAID THE BILL, walked out of the restaurant, crawled into her car, and headed north on the last leg of her trip back to Joe. She had just pulled into traffic when her cell vibrated.

"Hello?"

"Hey, Clara, it's Joe. Where are you?"

"I just had lunch at West Branch. Anything happening at home?"

"Yeah, big time. We just found out that it was Sammy the Grunt who hijacked Marie's car."

Clara gasped. "Sammy has Logan?"

"Not any more. Marie and Tom got their baby back this morning. Sammy left Marie's car in the mall's parking lot. He probably had no idea that Tom's kid was in the backseat."

"So Sammy's caught?"

"No, he just stole another car."

"Another car? So he's probably far away by now?"

"Aw, not really."

"So what's the story?"

"It's a long one, and I'll tell you when you get here."

"Marie must have been out of her mind. I feel badly that I wasn't there to support her. Who found Logan?"

"It's a long story, and I'll tell you when you get home."

"You and your long stories! I just can't imagine watching someone drive off with my baby. I hope Marie doesn't have any lasting psychological problems over this," Clara shuddered. "So if Sammy stole another car, does that mean he's still at large?"

"Yes, he's still out there."

"Come on, Joe, finish the story!"

"I'll finish it when you get home."

Clara snorted. "Anything else going on?"

"Well, the vineyard people are still camped at our house. You do remember inviting them just before you left to go looking for your lost dog?" His voice was loaded with sarcasm.

Clara heaved a huge sigh. "Yes, my love, I do remember agreeing to let them stay at our house, but that's not the same as inviting them. There's a difference, you know."

"The results are the same, aren't they?"

"Why don't you blame your best friend, Tom? He's the one who talked me into it. But enough of this. I want to hear more about Sammy. I don't want to wait until I get home. You said he's still at large?"

Joe signed. Bossy Clara, always pushing, pushing until she gets what she wants. "Yes, and probably on foot, unless he's hotwired another car. The car he switched to after dumping Marie's car was found a short distance away. It had run out of gas, and Sammy was nowhere to be found."

"Ouch. That's not good news. Please tell me that he didn't run out of gas anywhere near our house."

Joe was silent.

"So, that's why you didn't want to tell me the rest of the story!"

Joe didn't say anything.

"Aw , come on, Joe! You're teasing me, aren't you?"

"Teasing about Sammy? I don't think so."

"How close?"

"Well, since we all live within walking distance of each other, I can say that he's in our general area, but closer to Tom and Marie."

After a thoughtful pause, Clara said, "Syndee's tiny, and her bark is not much of a deterrent."

"Don't forget, Tom has a gun and we don't."

"Then I'm thankful that we have Lady, a really big dog."

"You're still several hours away. Drive carefully, please." As an afterthought, he added, "Clara, you have no idea how glad I am that you're coming home. I've missed you terribly."

He hung up before Clara could close her mouth.

DAMN, IT WAS COLD! Sammy pulled Dr. Bloom's winter jacket closer to his shivering body. It was just as cold inside the woodshed as it was outside. The only advantage of being inside was protection from the fast falling snow. The disadvantage was the thick spider webs that he kept running into. Did spiders hibernate in the winter, or were they somewhere in the web ready to spin a thread down to his head? With a feeling of panic, he shuddered as he swept a hand over his shaved head. He thought of the good doctor's warm house, the full pantry, and the stocked refrigerator. The image of the redhead cop who had kicked him out of the house was engraved in his brain. If circumstances ever presented an opportunity for another shot at payback….

But now was not the time to plan revenge; now was the time to figure out how he was going to survive. He stomped feet that he couldn't feel, and blew warm air on hands that were numb. Finding an unoccupied house shouldn't be too hard. Northern Michigan has many retired couples who spend the summers there, and the winters in the south. If he were going to stay alive, he needed to find one of those houses. But how was he going to do that? Anywhere he walked in the snow, he'd leave tracks behind. Just walking around a house, looking for a way to break into it, would leave incriminating footprints for anyone to follow.

Wait a minute. Wasn't it snowing hard enough to cover any footprint within minutes? When a quick look outside the shed assured him that his prints were already covered, he made a decision. It was now, not later. By morning, he'd be frozen if he didn't find a shelter better than the woodshed.

It was not a pleasant feeling having cold snow land on his shaved head. He could picture all the caps and hats Dr. Bloom had lined up in his closet, and fervently wished that he'd grabbed one when he'd left the warm house to find where the dentist kept food for the feeders. It was hard to believe that was just yesterday.

Trying to stay out of sight, he stuck to the back of the wooded properties as he made his way deeper into the subdivision. Dogs, aware of a walker, responded. From house to house, a steady chorus of barks traced his progress. Damn dogs! He hated all of them. To his dismay, he found himself coming to the end of the street. Had he missed the "Dead End" sign? How many blocks had he searched? Five? There were two houses left to check before the street ended and the woods began. He was looking for, but hadn't found, a house with clues that it was unoccupied, such as an unplowed driveway and closed blinds. He was getting desperate.

Sammy wasn't aware of it, but his ears were showing signs of frostbite. His beard was white from sticking snow, and the hair around his mouth was frozen stiff. He knew he was a dead man if he didn't find shelter…and soon.

His hands were numb, he couldn't feel his toes, and his nose was running. Panic was building, and his breathing was labored. Was this it? He had always thought that the end of his life would be accompanied by noise and violence. Freezing to death was such a wimpy way to go.

He'd lost track of the number of houses he'd checked. At each one he had crept as close as he could, listening for sound of activity; not one of them had been vacant. What were the chances that the last two would be any different? Maybe the street picked up on the other side of the woods. Would he survive if he explored that possibility? Violent shivers shook his body; he knew he was a dead man if he didn't find shelter soon. With a perverse sense of humor, he wondered if it really mattered where he froze to death.

The sound of either a radio or a television made short work of the one house. What was left was the last house next to the woods. That house could very well be his last chance of surviving. He noticed that while most of the window blinds were drawn, the open windows were dark. He wished he could go around to the front to see if the driveway was plowed, or if the door on the mailbox was securely held shut by a rubber band. That would be proof positive that the owners of the house were spending the winter somewhere where it was warm. But since he couldn't risk checking out the front of the house, he'd just have to take a chance. If it wasn't a vacant house and he was caught, then so be it. He'd be sent back to prison, but at least it would be warm in prison. It took another violent series of shivers to propel him into action. He was going to freeze to death if he didn't do something.

He was peeking into a back window of the house, trying to see around the edge of the drawn blind, when the sound of a door slamming shut made him drop to the ground. So, this wasn't a vacant house after all. The desperate tears that ran down his cheeks froze instantly. What now? Just crawl off and die? As he headed for the woods, curiosity got the better of him. What he saw when he turned around caused the wide smile on his face to crack the ice on his frozen beard. Was this for real? Was he hallucinating? He watched in absolute amazement as the redheaded cop stepped off the porch and headed for the garage. Sammy held his breath until the snitch backed the car out of the garage and drove away. This was the snitch's house! Could life get any better?

The sliding door was easy to remove from its track, and in a matter of minutes, he'd returned the door to its closed position; Sammy was standing inside the hated snitch's well-heated house. He closed his eyes and, for a brief moment, reveled in the warmth and in the anticipation of what he was going to do with the unexpected gift. Fantasies he'd designed while lying on his prison bunk were playing out in his head. He smiled. Yes, this was meant to be; there was no other explanation. The snitch's house had dropped into his hands like a nice ripe plum. Revenge was going to be slow and sweet; he'd take his time.

His smile vanished when his opened eyes landed on a dog bed and two bowls. Not another dog!

A female voice coming from another part of the house startled him. The snitch was married? A whole world of new ideas flooded his head. Figuring a wife into his revenge fantasies was going to take some planning...but not now. He needed to find a place to hide until his body quit shaking. And sleep. He needed to sleep.

Hearing footsteps coming his way, he ducked into the laundry room. The closet. He'd hide in the closet until his body was warm enough to think; his brain didn't work well when he was this cold. Just being inside the snitch's house was intoxicating, but he needed to be clear-headed when he planned the next move. If the female voice that he heard was truly the snitch's wife, he needed time to work her into his payback plan.

The closet in the laundry room was tiny. Sammy fit his body around a basket of dirty clothes, a large container of soap, and a vacuum cleaner. Even though he was uncomfortable in the cramped quarters, warmth was settling over his body, his eyes were heavy, his nose was running, and he could feel himself drifting off. He fought it for a bit, but soon sleep overcame him. Payback for the snitch and anyone else in the house would come soon enough. Using the sleeve of the snitch's jacket to wipe his nose gave him an odd sense of pleasure.

Sammy didn't dream very often, and when he did, the dreams were scary. Dreams of being cornered, dreams of trying to run from danger on legs that wouldn't move, dreams of looking into the eyes of a man that he had murdered, dreams of dying alone in prison...these were the ones he had grown accustomed to.

The dreams that he had while sleeping in the snitch's house were different and much scarier. They came from the part of Sammy's life that he had blocked off years ago, a life that had once held the promise of a good future. Flitting in and out of his dream was a young and very pretty girl whose smiling face was turned up, waiting for his kiss as he lifted her bridal veil. In the next scene, he saw that same face again, but this time there was no smile. In his dream, he remembered promises he had made to the pretty girl who had turned into someone with a perpetual frown. The last image he had of the tired-looking woman with calluses on her hands and knees was of her looking him in the eye as she quietly said goodbye, and then walked away.

Asleep in the snitch's closet, a solitary tear escaping from Sammy's closed eye roused him enough for him to bring up a hand to wipe it away. If he hadn't fallen back to sleep so quickly, he would have heard scratching noises coming from outside the closet door.

CHAPTER 40

OFFICER TOM ALLEN sat hunched over a cold cup of coffee and a half-eaten Danish roll at a back table in the Omelet Shop. His usual happy countenance was replaced by a worried look that matched his black-circled eyes. He was here because he needed to get away from the dark mood in his own house. The problem was Marie. His previously strong and confident wife was suddenly someone he didn't recognize.

Mitch Hatch stepped into the Omelet Shop and looked around for an empty table. The shop was doing a brisk breakfast business, and all the tables were filled. He was surprised to see Tom, in full uniform, alone at one of those tables. With Sammy still on the loose, shouldn't he have taken the day off work? It wasn't every day that a man's kidnapped son was returned home, safe and sound. With a concerned look on his face, Mitch made his way to the back table.

"Hi, Tom!"

Tom continued to stare into his cold coffee.

"Tom?" Mitch raised his voice.

Tom jumped. "Oh, hi, Mitch. You startled me!"

"You sure were deep in thought. Something bothering you? Is Logan really okay?"

"Oh, Logan's still sneezing and coughing, but since he kept all of us awake the night before, he probably slept through most of the ordeal. Being hungry and a little dehydrated were probably the only bad things that happened to him."

"I understand it would have been much worse if the crazy lady hadn't stepped in."

Tom shuddered. "I really can't let myself get into the 'what if' game because that's where Marie is, big time."

"What?"

"Marie is having a rough time. Of course she blames herself for letting Logan get kidnapped, but now that we've gotten him back, you'd think she'd be happy."

"She's not happy?"

"Mitch, she feels so much guilt! First, Logan caught his very first cold from her. and she feels badly about that. And then she keeps dwelling on all the 'what ifs'. It's true that if the homeless woman hadn't done the car thing, the story would have had a different ending. And if Sammy had known that it was my baby in the stolen car…well, I don't want to think about that, either, but Marie just can't shut down her imagination."

From the front of the restaurant, Fire Chief Joe Skinner spotted his buddies and headed their way. Being in a fine mood, he wanted to share his good news, but when he saw the serious looks on Tom and Mitch's faces, he slowed down.

"Hi, you two. Why the long faces?"

Both men look up at their smiling visitor.

"Well, you sure don't have a long face! What's your secret?" Mitch grinned as he pushed a chair in Joe's direction. "Sit down and cheer us up."

"Clara's on her way home!" Joe declared.

"Great news! But is she alone?" Tom asked.

"Yes, I'm afraid she didn't find her dog. Man, I'll be glad to see her, but I'm not looking forward to living with her. Remember what she was like the last time Lucky went AWOL?"

The other two men nodded.

"She still has Lady and Buddy," Tom remarked, and then he added, "Dogs can be such a comfort! Syndee seems to know that something's wrong with Marie. She won't leave her alone for a second."

Joe's head jerked. "Something wrong with Marie? Isn't she okay?"

"No, she's not okay," Tom sighed. "I didn't know my wife had such a wild imagination. She can't quit thinking of all the things that might have happened to Logan. They didn't happen, but they might have, and all of the scenarios she plays in her head have horrible endings. She insists that all the lights be off, all the blinds closed, and she's unplugged the phones. Our house is dark and silent. Every so often, she goes to the window, pulls back the shade, and peeks out. Who is she looking for?"

"Sammy?" suggested Mitch.

Tom looked up. "Isn't Sammy far away by now? He stole another car, didn't he?"

"Evidently you haven't heard," Mitch answered. "The car ran out of gas right after he stole it. You didn't know that?"

Tom's face turned white. "So Sammy's on foot? Where did his car run out of gas?"

Mitch cringed. "That's why we wondered why you were here and not at home with Marie and Logan. Sammy ran out of gas about five blocks from your house," he replied softly.

Tom jumped to his feet so fast his almost empty cup of coffee turned upside down on top of the partially eaten Danish. "I shouldn't have left Marie alone! Sammy will do anything to stay out of prison, and that makes him very dangerous. Have my neighbors been warned?"

Mitch nodded, "Yes, but if Marie has unplugged your phones, she'd have no way to get the message."

Tom ran out of the Omelet Shop.

———————

"MARIE!" TOM YELLED, as he burst through the door. "Where are you?"

A weak and subdued noise came from the back area of the house. Tom raced to their bedroom, stood in the doorway, and surveyed the scene. Syndee was curled up beside Marie's pillow-covered head, and the rest of her was just a long lump under the covers.

"Hon, this is where I left you this morning. Haven't you gotten out of bed?"

A muffled voice came from under the pillow. "I had to feed and change Logan, didn't I?"

"Why is your head under the pillow?" Tom asked gently. It pained him to see his strong and capable wife reduced to this. The "what ifs" had to stop.

"Because of the scratching."

"Scratching?"

"Yes, the scratching. Syndee kept going into the laundry room and scratching on the closet door."

"Why was she scratching?"

"Who knows?"

"Well, she's not doing it now."

"That's because I closed the laundry room door."

"Marie, you know there's something wrong with the latch on that door. It doesn't stay shut."

She actually had a chuckle in her voice when she answered. "It does if you lock it!"

"Good thinking!" Tom was encouraged by her chuckle. Could it be that she was ready to put her guilt feelings to rest? Too bad that what he had to tell her just might set her off again.

"Uh, Marie, since Syndee isn't scratching, why is your head still under the pillow?"

"I kinda like it under here," was her muffled reply.

Tom sighed. "Now, Marie, I'm going to tell you something that's going to upset you."

Marie threw off the pillow and sat up. "I don't think you can tell me anything that will upset me any more than I already am."

"I think I can. There's a good chance that Sammy is loose in our neighborhood."

"What?" Marie yelled. "That can't be! I was told he stole a car when he left mine behind in the mall."

"Well, he did. But the car ran out of gas almost immediately after he stole it. The car was found close to our subdivision, but there was no sign of Sammy. Since no one has reported their car being stolen, there's a good possibility that Sammy's on foot, probably looking for shelter in somebody's house. He's gonna need it; the temperature has dropped and it's snowing pretty hard."

"Sammy's out there somewhere? Maybe in our backyard? Oh, Tom, get me out of here!"

"That's exactly what I have in mind. How long will it take you to clean up? You're looking pretty scruffy, you know."

Marie shook her head. "I've been wallowing in self pity long enough. I'll jump into the shower while you grab baby and dog supplies. We can be out of here in thirty minutes!"

With a relieved sigh, Tom muttered, "That my Marie!"

———————

IT WAS HOURS later when Sammy finally woke up. He opened his eyes and saw nothing. Nothing? Was he blind? He tried to move, but objects seemed to get in his way. His one arm was asleep, and his legs were tangled with a thick cord. Slowly, he remembered. He was in a closet in the redheaded snitch's house. That was good, but why was it so dark?

Cautiously, he pushed on the folding closet door. Even with the door open, it was still pitch black in the room. He remembered the vacuum cleaner he had fitted his body around; that would explain the cord tangling his legs.

He tried to be quiet, but a sneeze and extracting his body from the closet made a lot of noise. Holding his breath, he waited for several minutes, expecting the cop to come busting into the room. When nothing happened, he stood upright, and stretched.

It was so dark, it was hard to think. Dare he switch on the light? No, that wasn't a good idea. Maybe somewhere in the house there was a nightlight. Yes, that's what he'd do; he'd leave the laundry room and look for the room with a nightlight. The dog! He'd almost forgotten about the dog. What was he going to do about a barking dog? Maybe he should stay where he was until morning. Yes, that's what he'd do, but finding the door was still a good idea. He tried to remember his journey through the house after he'd gained entrance.

Stumbling around, he bumped into a washer, a dryer, something that felt like an ironing board, and then a wall. Following the wall, his hands landed on the light switch. Resisting the urge to flip it, his hands kept moving. Ah, yes! A doorknob! Could he sneak a little peek without alerting the dog?

It took a few seconds of trying to turn the knob before reality hit. He was locked in.

Sammy froze. They knew.

His mouth was bone dry, and his heart was jumping out of his chest. How long were they going to keep him in here before confronting him? No, no, this couldn't be happening. Fate had brought him to this house for a reason. He hadn't even been looking for the snitch's house. It had found him!

Since they knew he was here, there was no sense in being quiet or stumbling around in the dark. His finger hesitated for a moment on the switch; was this really a good idea? Wait a minute! They might know someone was in here, but did they know who they'd locked up?

Of course they knew.

He shrugged and flipped the switch. Light flooded the small windowless room. When he saw that the door was the only way out of the room, he felt the walls closing in on him; was this his new cell?

He held his breath and listened. Were they standing on the other side of the door, waiting for him to do something? Where was the dog?

Well, if that's the game they were playing, so be it. He emptied the dirty clothesbasket, turned it over, and with a resigned look on his face, he sat down facing the door…and sneezed.

So this is how it was going to end…not with a bang, but with a sneeze and a whimper. The taste of defeat was bitter; the snitch had won.

CHAPTER 41

CLARENCE WAS HAVING a hard time believing Joe.

"You're tellin' me that the baldheaded bearded man that got out of his car and kicked Buddy was Sammy the Grunt? I don't think so!"

"Believe it, Clarence."

Clarence's face blanched.

"What's wrong?"

"I shook my fist at him!"

"So?"

"You really don't know Sammy, do you?"

"Well, can't say that I do. You know him up close and personal, don't you?"

"Too close and too personal. The last time I saw him, he was shootin' at me. The only reason he didn't kill me was because I slipped and fell. Good thing the state police showed up."

"Albert and Sarah have told some pretty scary stories. Living under the same roof with Sammy had to be frightening."

"I have nightmares," Clarence confessed. "But if I have Buddy in bed with me, I don't."

"Buddy chases away the boogeyman?" laughed Joe.

"You can laugh, Joe, but if you knew the real boogeyman like I do, you'd have nightmares, too." Clarence stepped closer to Joe and whispered, "I pulled the trigger twice."

"On a gun? You pulled the trigger on a gun twice?"

Clarence nodded his head.

"Who were you trying to shoot?"

"Sammy."

"Why haven't I heard this story?"

"Because it makes us all look bad."

"Bad as in…?"

"Bad as in not havin' enough guts to shoot the bastard when we had the chance! There are a lot more stories that they haven't told. I relive them in my nightmares."

"Clarence, if Buddy helps you sleep at night, then…."

The doorbell rang. Joe's face lit up. Could it be Clara?

Before he even got to the door, it flew open and the entire snow-covered Allen household, along with suitcases, a bulging diaper bag, and a container of dog food, rushed into the foyer. Immediately, Syndee took off, looking for Buddy and Lady.

Joe raised his eyebrows, "Yes?"

Marie burst into tears. "Is Clara back? I need my big sister!"

"SLOW DOWN, MOLLY, and say it again," Mitch pleaded. "What's the problem with Agda?"

Molly took a deep breath and repeated herself. "Agda is freaking out! She watched the news and heard that an escaped convict was last seen in a nearby neighborhood."

"Sammy's on foot, and I can see why she might be frightened. What's going on in your office?"

"Well, I do have an appointment with a transferee, but the way it's snowing out there, I wouldn't be surprised if he calls to cancel it."

"So, what does Agda want to do?"

"She just doesn't want to be alone with the girls and the twins."

"Are you thinking about Joe and Clara's house? Hey, did you hear that Clara is on her way home?"

"With Lucky?"

"Unfortunately, not with the dog."

Molly groaned. "We both know what kind of a mood Clara will be in. I'm not looking forward to having her glum face back in my office!"

"Well, since you're tied up at the office and I can't take off work to stay home with them, do you think Joe would mind if I showed up at his door with Agda, the girls, the twins, and Rosie, the pup?"

"Isn't Joe at the fire station?"

"No, he's taking a vacation day. I saw him at the Omelet Shop this morning. It's going to be interesting to see how he greets Clara when she does get home."

"Why is that?"

"He really wants her home! He's been pining around like a lost little boy. It's the first time they've been apart since they've been married. On the other hand, he's *really* upset that she left him with the vineyard people."

"Tom talked her into that."

"Well, she did agree to take them, but then she left to find Lucky."

"Hon, don't even try to understand Clara's love for that dog, and if Joe is jealous of Lucky, I can see why he would be."

Mitch cleared his throat. "Tell you what. I'll go home and pick up Agda, the pup, and the kids, and drop them off at Joe and Clara's house. Why don't you go there after you're through with your transferee, and I'll stop in after work?"

"Sounds like a plan. Oh, my transferee just walked in!"

"Bye."

———

LUCKY WAS GETTING weary just trying to stay on the trailer. Without the harness strapped around him, every time the car changed lanes or made a quick stop, he had to dig in his claws to keep from sliding off. His muscles were quivering with the effort.

He was reveling in familiar smells and feelings. His doggy sense told him that not only were they traveling in the right direction, he could see his most favorite person in the car ahead.

He could feel it in his bones; he was going home.

SOMEONE SNEEZED.

Sammy woke up with a jerk, and frantically looked around. There was no one in the room with him, so if someone sneezed, it must have been him. How long had he been sitting on the upside-down laundry basket? And why did he feel so lousy, he wondered while wiping his nose on Dr. Bloom's coat sleeve. He had no watch, and since the room was windowless, he didn't have a clue. What kind of game were they playing? Were they waiting for him to beg?

The situation was puzzling. They must have known he was hiding in the laundry room. There was no other reason for them to have locked the door. But why was it so silent on the other side?

He made his way to the door, put his ear against it, and listened. Nothing. Dare he knock? What did he have to lose? One way or another, they had him trapped.

He tried a few gentle taps. When nothing happened, the gentle taps turned into louder ones. Eventually, he was pounding on the door.

Reality hit; no one was home. Did they leave because they knew he was hiding in their house? Sammy shook his head. No, if they had known, by now, the house would be surrounded, and a cop would be yelling into a bullhorn for him to exit the house with his hands up; that was not happening.

Did he dare he hope that all was not lost?

With a running start, his shoulder hit the flimsy door with the faulty latch; the door splintered and flew open.

When a quick search of the house validated his suspicion that no one was home, he headed to the kitchen.

The hastily made sandwich tasted as good as a Thanksgiving dinner. What was left of a gallon of milk found its way past his sensitive teeth and down his throat, straight from the jug.

A sneeze and a glance out the window at the deepening snow reminded him that he needed warmer clothes. He set aside a pair of Tom's boots, a down-filled jacket, a woolen hat to cover his shaved head, and a pair of warm ski gloves. He didn't need them now, but for once, he had time to plan ahead.

While the family was away, Sammy felt free to search the house looking for objects to aid him in his fantasy-fueled payback session with the snitch.

CHAPTER 42

THE BLACK SKY and the rapidly falling snow added to Clara's growing apprehension. The closer she got to her destination, the more agitated she became. Joe was really upset with her. She had grown used to the underlying sound of unconditional love when he talked to her. Now, when she answered her cell phone, she didn't recognize the harsh voice on the other end. Had she ruined the wonderful and magical element that had been in their marriage?

Tears ran down her face as she tried to put herself in Joe's shoes. How would she feel if he'd left her with a house full of people and had gone after an animal? An animal? Lucky was much more than just an animal. Joe knew that, didn't he?

She paused in her angst to speed up the windshield wipers.

Lucky was truly gone. How was she going to go on living, pretending that everything was fine, when it really wasn't? Just thinking of living in a world without Lucky brought a new onslaught of tears. Quickly, she swiped her coat sleeve over her eyes. She was driving in a snowstorm, for heaven's sake! The last thing she needed was blurred vision.

Molly was angry with her, too. But why should she be? Hadn't she held the business together when Molly was off all those months before and after she'd had twins? She'd taken just a few *days* off to look for Lucky, not *months*!

Well, Joe would just have to get over it, and so would Molly. If they didn't understand why she had to go and look for her lost dog, then so be it. The love she felt for that smelly, furry animal was deep and unexpected. Could anyone explain love?

The further north she drove, the colder it got. She watched the car's outside thermometer slide down to a single digit. The wipers were losing their battle to clear the rapidly piling snow on her windshield.

Her mind drifted off her lost dog and settled on the lost baby. According to Joe, Logan was safely back home, unharmed. What a horrific experience that must have been for Marie! Comparing her lost dog to a lost baby wasn't even possible. How Marie must have hurt! Clara cringed just thinking about it. When Marie had needed her big sister, Clara hadn't been around.

There was very little traffic on the snow-covered road. Carefully following the signs, she exited I-75. The trailer fishtailed as she turned onto a smaller county road.

She was almost home.

On the trailer behind Clara's car, Lucky was holding on for dear life with paws that were nothing but frozen balls of ice. Several inches of snow covered his black fur. He was freezing, he was hungry, and his muscles were tired from the constant battle to stay on the trailer.

SAMMY ROAMED THROUGH the empty house, looking for hiding places and weapons. Not only had he found a box of tissues for his running nose, he'd found a safe that probably had the snitch's service weapon, but he didn't waste any time playing with the dial. What were the odds he'd stumble onto the combination? He finally settled on a sharp kitchen knife. Pleased with his choice, he positioned himself in a secluded spot by the door; they wouldn't see him before he pounced.

Where were they?

By the time an hour had passed, Sammy was not only stiff from hiding, he was bored. He was finding it hard to maintain the level of hatred toward the snitch that he'd need if he wanted to accomplish even one of the payback fantasies. Droopy eyes and a growling stomach were replacing the burning revenge feelings.

Did he dare make coffee?

While the coffee was perking, another search of the refrigerator produced the remains of a casserole.

Sammy was sitting at the table, enjoying the reheated casserole and the fresh pot of coffee, when a ringing phone shattered the silence of the house. Startled, Sammy choked on a mouthful of coffee. He was still coughing when the answering machine kicked in.

"Hi, Tom, it's Mom," he heard.

He'd run into Tom's mother before. She was the one who was sitting in the Sunday open house, the one where he'd stabbed her son, the snitch.

"I'm surprised that you're not home. What are you doing out in weather like this? Oh, there I go again, sounding like a mother! Sorry about that."

There was a pause while she took a deep breath. "I'm just concerned about Marie. I can't begin to imagine what she felt as she watched her car being hijacked with Baby Logan in the back seat. Tom, you must have been wild with fear when you found out that it was Sammy the Grunt who stole her car!"

Silence.

"Well, call me when you get home."

Sammy's head jerked. That was the snitch's car? And the snitch's baby was in the back seat?

With a cry of anguish, all the pent-up anger returned in full force. What he could have done had he known that he had the snitch's baby!

It would have been a payback that would have been way beyond any fantasy he'd dreamed up in prison.

With a wild sweep of his arm, he cleared the table of dishes. The china shattering when it hit the floor was a sweet sound, as was the thud when he smashed the baby's crib against the wall, and the crunch of glass on a framed wedding picture that he ground under his foot; exhaustion was the only thing that made him stop.

Breathing hard, he stood in the middle of the trashed house; the extent of the damage surprised even him. He'd had the perfect payback handed to him, and he'd flubbed it. If only he had known! But he hadn't. Waves of pure hate were making his body shake and his heart pound. Where were they? He needed to hurt the meddlesome cop who constantly got in his way, and the baby was a sure way to do that. But to do anything, he had to find them.

The phone rang. Sammy waited to hear if the caller would leave a message.

"Hi, it's Mitch."

Sammy's ears twitched. He'd had a few run-ins with the detective.

"I hope that since you didn't answer the phone means you've taken your family to a safe place. I'm about to join my family at Joe and Clara's house. The vineyard people are still there. It will be good to see Albert and Clarence again. Hmmm…maybe that's where you are? Bye."

Fortified with a cold bottle of beer, Sammy pushed the remains of a smashed potted plant off the sofa, and sat down to think. Had the caller just told him where the snitch and his family were? At Joe and Clara's house?

With closed eyes, the better to think, he tried to remember details from the past, details of his life before the big dog had brought him down in the vineyard.

Oh, yes. Clara was the owner of the big dog. He hated that dog! She was also the one he used to call Miss Piggy when he visited her at a real estate office…Allen Real Estate, if he remembered correctly. He didn't remember Joe, though. Wait a minute. Wasn't there a fire truck and a firefighter mentioned in the newspaper article? The guards had delighted in rubbing his nose in the headlines and the vineyard picture of the big dog sitting on top of him. Could Joe be that fireman?

A quick look in a kitchen drawer produced a phone book, and a quick call to the fire department gave him the name of the fire chief: Joseph Skinner. Sammy grinned as he looked up Joe's address.

While he was in the kitchen looking for the phone book, he opened the refrigerator and grabbed another beer.

Detective Mitch, he knew, was involved in solving the McGuire Alley murders that had sent him to prison. The vineyard people were fresh in his mind. He certainly needed to punish Albert and Clarence for all the things they had done to him. His hand automatically went up to a still-fresh scar on his head. Sarah needed a payback for hitting him on the head with the poker.

If he had figured it out right, all the people from his past who had participated one way or another in his downfall were under one roof.

It was after the fourth beer that the bright idea had popped into his not-so-used-to-alcohol brain.

Why not pay them all a visit?

CHAPTER 43

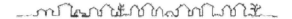

AS JOE LOOKED OVER his crowded living room, a quote made by a famous baseball player came to mind: "It's like déjà vu all over again." All that was missing was the sound of the running generator and sleeping bags…and, of course, Clara and Lucky. Clara should be pulling in any hour now, and Lucky? Only God knew where the dog was.

Marie, Sarah, and Molly were in the kitchen working together; the argument that had split the cooks during the power failure evidently had been forgotten. Joe didn't know what supplies the women had to work with. Since he hadn't been spending much time at home, Albert and Sarah had been doing the shopping.

Clarence was playing with Rosie and Buddy, completely ignoring Syndee, the pretend dog. All that was missing was the evil cat, Blackie.

It was hard to hear the doorbell over the hubbub of voices and the barking of the dogs, but the sound finally got to Joe. He was almost afraid to open the door.

Standing on the porch was Peggy, the mother of Tom and Molly, and behind her were Mitch's parents, Marilyn and Richard.

Before Joe could say anything, Richard cleared his throat. "Uh, Peggy called us. She was scared. Someone told her that Sammy the Grunt was running loose, and she didn't want to be alone in her big house."

Peggy's curly head was bobbing up and down, agreeing with what Richard was telling Joe. "I asked them to bring me here because I felt so safe when I was with you during the power failure. I do hope that wasn't presumptuous of me."

Hiding crossed fingers behind his back, Joe lied. "No, no, nothing of the kind! All of you, please come in. You certainly should feel safe here, Peggy. I think half the population of the town is already inside."

Mitch looked surprised when he saw the newcomers. "Mom and Dad! What brings you here?"

Richard did nothing but nod his head at Peggy. "She asked us to bring her here, so we did."

Noticing the stiff way his dad was standing, holding his coat shut with both hands, Mitch narrowed his eyes and asked, "Dad, do you have something under your coat?"

Marilyn whirled around. "You didn't!"

"Didn't what, Mom?" Mitch asked.

Marilyn grabbed her husband, "Richard, is that Blackie under your coat?"

When Richard backed up, he not only lost his balance, he also lost his grip on the cat. With a hiss and flailing claws, Blackie jumped out of Richard's arms. The pups, which had smelled cat stink the moment Blackie had been carried through the door, were ready. As soon as Blackie's feet hit the floor, they were on his tail.

The next time Blackie was seen, he was high above the crowd, balancing on Clara's drapery rods.

Joe just shook his head; it really was déjà vu all over again.

———

SAMMY WAS FEELING no pain. Giggling to himself, he staggered to the bedroom where there was a full-length mirror. Tom's winter clothes fit him perfectly. The reflected image of him in the snitch's clothes prompted him to hold up the almost-empty beer bottle in a toast to himself. He winked at his reflection; revenge was going to be *so* sweet!

Before leaving the warm house, he struggled to check his pockets. Not being able to stand too steadily, his hands were having trouble finding them. That brought on more giggles. Not knowing what he was going to run into, he'd looked for anything that might come in handy. One pocket he'd stuffed with tissues. In another, he had the knife, along with duct tape, rope, matches, a flashlight, and in case he should run into an unfriendly dog, he'd grabbed a handful of treats. The neighborhood seemed to be filled with dogs, if all the barking he'd heard meant anything.

Assured that he hadn't forgotten anything, he opened the door to step outside, and then paused. He needed another beer.

After putting a bottle in his hip pocket, he noticed that there was only one beer left in the refrigerator. Hey, didn't he have another hip pocket? Sammy giggled as he struggled to wedge it in. Now where had he put the bottle opener? Ah, yes. It should be on the floor, along with everything else from a drawer he had dumped. Crawling on his hands and knees, he worked his way to the pile and found the opener. Unfortunately, he had left one cabinet drawer pulled out, and when he tried to stand, he whacked his head on it. Falling backward, he lost his balance and flopped to the floor, landing on his butt. Sammy giggled. That must have been a funny sight to see. He pictured in his mind what he must have looked like when he fell on his butt, and that brought on more giggles. Wait! Had he broken the two bottles of beer that he had put in his hip pockets? The very thought that landing in his butt might have broken them was so funny, he ended up rolling on the floor, holding his side. When he noticed that he'd rolled in a pile of flour and sugar he had dumped on the floor, he laughed so hard, he could feel warm pee running down his leg.

The urge just to stay where he was and take a little nap was strong. He was drunk, but not quite drunk enough to forget the mission that didn't seem quite so important anymore. He didn't know why, but a lot of his heated anger had dissipated. Why couldn't he just stay here in the nice warm house? No, no, he couldn't let all those people get away with what they had done to him...especially the snitch. Just the thought of the redheaded cop spurred him into action. With much effort, he pushed himself off the floor and onto his feet...unfortunately, in the middle of the sugar spill. His feet flew out from under him.

As he lay on his back, looking up at the ceiling, he marveled at what a good time he was having. He hadn't laughed like this in years. Moments such as this needed to be celebrated!

He drank his next-to-last beer.

ICY PAWS WERE making the job of staying on the slippery trailer almost impossible; Lucky's legs were shaking from the effort. He would have given up many miles ago, except in his dreams that person behind the wheel of the car ahead of him was always the person who was calling his name.

His eyes were trying to close. Cold, tired, and hungry, his body was shutting down.

Against his will, Lucky fell asleep.

SAMMY WAS AMAZED at the information that he'd found in the phone book. It was on one of the maps in the front of the book that he had pinpointed Tom's house where he was now, and the directions to take him to Joe and Clara's house. It wasn't really very far, and Tom's clothes would keep him warm.

Too bad he had to stick to the back of the properties. The accumulated winter snow made walking difficult, but it did make a soft cushion when he fell...which he did...several times. In the snow behind him, Sammy was leaving a wavering trail and an occasional snow angel image. He couldn't remember when he'd had such a good time. After each fall, he checked to make sure the bottle in his hip pocket hadn't broken.

Walking against the cold wind was making his eyes water. What had he done with good old Dr. Bloom's sunglasses? The wind kept trying to blow the wet and limp map out of his hand. A fast gust of wind had already made Joe and Clara's address disappear. Sammy giggled, but he didn't worry. He'd find the house.

CHAPTER 44

THE CROWD IN Joe's house had mingled over the soup and sandwich meal the women had whipped together. Clarence was entertaining the children with tricks he'd taught the puppies, while the two women with babies had their heads together, swapping Sammy the Grunt stories. Sarah grimaced when she told Marie the story about Sammy actually touching her baby. When Marie heard that Sarah had been cuffed when this had happened, she reached out a sympathetic hand and touched her. Sarah shuddered when Marie described the scene when her car had been hijacked with Logan in the backseat. That was a story that sent fear into a mother's heart. The men were in the corner of the room, talking in hushed voices. If Sammy did show up, how were they going to defend themselves?

"How many guns do we have among the three of us?" asked Detective Mitch. "I have mine. Joe, do you have a gun?"

Joe shook his head. "I had one, but Clara made me get rid of it."

"How about you, Tom? I know you had it this morning when we saw you at the Omelet Shop."

"I wasn't thinking straight, guy. The first thing I always do when I walk into the house from work is to put my gun in the safe...it's a habit. And I'm afraid that's what I did today. So, no, I don't have my gun with me. Do you think I should go home and get it?"

Mitch nodded. "I think you should."

Tom pulled his car keys out of his pocket and headed for the door.

"Tell Marie I'll be right back!" he yelled over his shoulder.

Tom had to brush several inches of snow off his car before he could drive it. When he finally pulled into the street, his tires whined while trying to get traction on the deep-snow-covered pavement. Another winter storm was in full swing.

One glance at his house as he pulled into the driveway told him all was not well…the front door was standing wide open.

Without a gun in his hand, Tom felt naked as he approached his house. Should he call for backup? Frantically searching his pockets, he tried to remember the last time he'd seen his cell phone. Whenever that was, it didn't matter now, because he didn't have it. After a moment of hesitation, he cautiously entered.

For a moment, he froze, not willing to believe what his eyes were seeing. In the middle of the kitchen floor, smashed dishes, along with flour, salt, and sugar were mixed with emptied jars of baby food. Pieces of Logan's broken crib lay in the middle of the mess. Looking into the living room, he could see that Marie's plants had been broken off and the dirt piled on the sofa. What maniac had been in his house? He stood in front of the smashed laundry room door and didn't want to believe what it meant.

After a quick search of the house convinced him that he was alone, he called his station and explained what had happened. Telling his superior that he needed to be with his family, he left him Joe's landline phone number in case they wanted to contact him.

A trip to the safe to retrieve his gun, and then it was back to Joe's house. He was wondering how he was going to break the latest news to Marie.

———

CLARA TURNED THE heater up as far as it would go. The windshield wipers were struggling, and the temperature on her outside thermometer read zero. Would this trip ever end? Leery as she was about facing Joe, his wrath would be a welcome relief from the hours of driving through the storm. It had become a constant fight to stay on the road; the sliding trailer hooked to her car didn't help. If only Lucky were on that trailer! But he wasn't, and she had to accept the fact that she probably would never see her dog again. She fought the threatening tears that would make driving impossible. *Think about something else,* she told herself. Buddy. She'd think about that cute little puppy that looked so much like his dad.

Lost in thought, she almost missed her next turn. Even though she gently eased on the brakes, the car still fishtailed. The trailer whipped from side to side, making it hard for her to complete the turn. Fortunately, since she was the only car on the road, her vehicle straightened out without running into anything. This was the road that would take her home; she was almost there. She sighed in relief.

Clara never saw the snow-covered mound that slid off the trailer and disappeared into the snow-filled ditch.

CHAPTER 45

EVEN THOUGH IT WAS freezing cold, Sammy's effort to walk in the deep snow was making him sweat. How could he be hot when it was so cold? Toying with the thought of discarding some of his warm clothes, he settled on drinking the last cold beer that he'd safely stored in his hip pocket.

Getting the beer out was easy enough once he took of his gloves. When fumbling through all his many pockets didn't produce the bottle opener, he emptied them all onto a snow bank. The opener was the last object in the last pocket. Wasn't that the way it always worked?

When he found the trunk of a tree big enough to block off the wind, he sat down, opened the beer, and felt the cool liquid run down his throat. It had been years since he'd had the opportunity to have one beer, and here he was, free as a bird, drinking his sixth one.

Leaning his back against the tree, he closed his eyes and thought how great freedom was, and how sad he was going to be when it ended...and he knew it would end. The things he had done since the day of the trip to the dentist ran through his mind. He had killed the man driving the car he had hijacked, but he hadn't killed the dentist. That death shouldn't be held against him. He had just learned that when he hijacked one of the cars, there had been a baby in the backseat. Does it count as a kidnapping if you didn't know the kid was in the car? Oh, yes. Don't forget the vineyard people. What would they charge him for on that? No one had died, but he had held them prisoner.

No matter how he figured the angles, it was not going to be pleasant when he finally was caught...but before that happened, he would finish one last bit of business. Right after a little nap, he'd find the house where all those people were, and he'd show them. He'd block all the doors, and then he'd burn the house down, that's what he'd do! With one match, he'd settle all the old scores, and then he wouldn't mind if they caught him and put him back into prison. That made him think of the matches that he'd need to set fire to the house...when he found it. Which pocket were they in? Oh, that's right; he'd emptied his pockets when he was looking for the opener. But that was okay; he knew where they were. He'd worry about that right after a little nap.

A sneeze interrupted his descent into sleep. While fishing a tissue out of his pocket, he wondered if he was coming down with something; his face felt hot when he touched it. Now that he was wide-awake, he thought again, how wonderful it was to be out of prison; any day that he wasn't behind bars was a good day. He'd have to remember this moment, because he knew that once he was back in prison, his jailers would see to it that he'd never have another chance to escape, that meant he'd never again sit under a tree, and that never again would he drink a beer.

Despite the nerves in his broken front teeth objecting, he took a deep breath of the clean, cold air of freedom, and fell asleep.

JARRED AWAKE BY the soft-snowy landing, Lucky shook the snow off his black fur and crawled out of the ditch. What had happened to the trailer? He looked around, confused for a moment, and then he turned his nose in the right direction, and started walking.

His doggy sense told him the way to home was straight ahead.

———————

WITH MIXED FEELINGS, Clara turned onto her street; she'd made it home. Just a few more blocks to go, and then she'd pull into her driveway. What were her chances that Joe would come out to greet her with a smile and a hug?

Why were there so many cars parked around her house? Joe wouldn't be having a party without her, would he? Someone was even parked in her driveway.

Wait a minute. Could there have been another power outage? A selfish thought ran through her head. Maybe they should just get rid of the generator if this was going to happen every time the power went out.

She changed her mind as her friends poured out of the opened front door to welcome her. These were the very people her selfish thought would have kept away.

The last person out of the house was Joe. Standing alone, he watched Clara accepting the hugs and the sympathetic murmurings about her missing dog. At last, she stopped in front of him.

"Joe?" she whispered.

The contrite look on Clara's face stopped Joe from venting his pent-up feelings about his playing second fiddle to a dog. He even surprised himself when he grabbed her in a bear hug.

"Clara! God, how I've missed you!"

Held back tears streamed down her face. "Oh, Joe! I was so scared! You were angry with me when we talked on the phone, and I thought...I thought...."

Joe never heard what she thought, because he kissed her.

CHAPTER 46

LOST IN THOUGHT, CLARA walked through her house, touching things that were precious to her, things that made her house a home. Gone for such a short time, but so much had happened in those days! From the kitchen, she could hear apprehension in the voices of her friends; how safe were they? It wasn't a power outage that had brought them together, but a mutual fear of Sammy the Grunt. And until he was caught, they probably would stay camped in her house.

The walk took her past walls that were covered with framed newspaper articles, in chronological order, that told of Lucky's claim to fame. Standing quietly in her living room, she gazed at the picture of Lucky lying on top of Santa Claus. That year, the Christmas parade had been canceled because Lucky had attacked Santa.

Sammy the Grunt, or what you could see of him, was in the next framed picture. Lucky had run him down in the vineyard and sat on him until help had arrived.

Painful memories brought tears to her eyes as she hastily passed by the next picture. Lucky had flirted with death when he had thrown his body over Joe, protecting him from an exploding bomb. The picture showed Lucky with large areas of burned skin. Shuddering, she moved on.

The framed picture next in line featured Lucky, along with a small dog that had all the fur chewed off the back of her neck. Clara smiled when she remembered that the owner of pedigreed Syndee wouldn't have anything more to do with a dog that had Lucky's mongrel spit all over her. Syndee now lived with Marie, Tom, and Logan.

Joe had pleaded with her not to put the next picture on the wall, but Clara had insisted. After all, it was their wedding picture. Lucky had walked her down the aisle...that was all he was supposed to do. But when he had stood up on his hind legs just when Joe, with closed eyes, had leaned over to kiss his bride, he'd kissed Lucky's furry face. The photographer had captured the moment.

The sixth picture wasn't from the newspaper. Clara had taken the picture when Lucky had returned home after being missing for many days. When he'd come back, he was not alone. With him had been a female dog and two puppies that looked just like him. The picture she had taken captured Lucky and his new family.

During that time when he had been gone, Clara had fallen apart. Looking back, she knew her behavior had been extreme, but her grief over the missing dog was real. Why she loved Lucky so much was a question she didn't even try to answer; she just did. She had searched, cried, prayed, and was inconsolable. The thought that she might never see him again had threatened to undo her. But he had returned that time.

The only room that she hadn't visited was the dogs' addition. The two pups, Buddy and Rosie and the laid-back lazy Lady probably would be sleeping. But Lucky, the love of her life, would not be in there, and probably never would be, ever again. She sucked in her breath, and dared the tears to come. Hardening her resolve not to fall apart and embarrass herself, as she had done the last time he had gone missing, she squared her shoulders and wiped away one rebel tear.

A sob escaped her as she turned away.

———————

WHY IS IT that when more than two people are in a house, they gravitate to the kitchen? Be it a party, or be it a group of friends huddled together for protection, they always seem to congregate in the kitchen, around the coffeepot. There weren't enough chairs for everyone in Clara's kitchen, so those who didn't have a chair were leaning against the breakfast bar.

While Tom was standing by the kitchen phone, waiting for a call from the station, Marie was sitting at the table, talking to the other women. Watching his beloved Marie's animated face as she interacted with them, and remembering how devastated she'd been when Logan had been kidnapped, Tom's resolve to find the man who had caused her so much grief intensified.

Tom hadn't told Marie about their trashed home. The call he was waiting for would verify that the fingerprints from his house were the same as the ones they'd found in the dentist's house. He had no doubt that it was Sammy who had come looking for him, and if the extent of the destruction matched Sammy's anger, then it was a good thing Sammy hadn't found him.

When the phone rang, Tom was waiting. The room quieted down, as they watched his face, trying to get a clue as to what was making him so agitated.

"So?" Mitch asked when Tom put down the phone. "What did they tell you?"

Tom took a deep breath and shuddered. "That son of a bitch was hiding in our laundry room."

"It was Sammy?" Mitch asked.

"Yes, it was. Is anyone surprised?"

Marie cried. "Wait a minute! Hiding in our laundry room? When was he doing that?"

"Probably when you and Logan were home alone."

Marie's face turned white. "How do you figure that?"

"Remember, when I came home, you were in bed with a pillow over your head?"

Marie caught her breath. "Syndee kept scratching at the closet door in the laundry room, and I put a pillow over my head…" She covered her mouth with a hand. "Do you mean Sammy was hiding in the closet when I locked the laundry room door?"

"Had to be. When I went back for the gun, I thought as much when I saw that the laundry room door was smashed. They think he got into the house by taking the sliding door off its track. That's easy enough to do, if you know how."

"How do they know he was in the closet?"

"Remember it was snowing quite hard last night, and the snow he dragged in on his boots left a big puddle where it melted. And objects in the closet had been pushed out, too. Looks like he just curled up in there and took a nap."

"So when he woke up and found the door locked, he smashed the door to get out?"

"Looks like it."

Marie shuddered.

"Uh… honey, the door is not the only thing that he smashed. He, uh, he kinda, uh, he kinda…." Tom sputtered and stopped.

"Kinda did what, Tom? What else did he do?"

"Uh, he…he kinda smashed up a few more things." The startled look on Marie's face caused him to add in a rush, "But you don't have to worry. The guys from the station are taking care of it."

Marie looked at him with questions in her eyes, but he just shook his head. Translated, that look meant *don't push it*. She nodded.

"Did they find anything else?" Joe inquired.

"They found Dr. Bloom's coat and probably his boots, too, but the boots didn't have his name on them; the coat did," Tom replied.

"What does that mean?" inquired Mitch. "You didn't find him in the house, so what did he wear to go back outside? It's zero out there!"

Scratching on the door sent Clara to open it. The two puppies flew into the room, bringing snow and cold air with them.

Mitch yelled at their pup as she ran across the room, "Come back here, Rosie! What do you have in your mouth?"

"My hat!" hollered Tom. "That's my hat! Where in the hell did Rosie find my hat?"

The room grew silent.

"Now we know what Sammy put on when he left Dr. Bloom's winter clothes behind."

"My clothes," Tom sputtered. "That...that bastard is wearing my clothes."

"Rosie," Clara picked up the pup and looked into her eyes. "Rosie, where did you find the hat?"

The pup squirmed out of her arms, but not before she gave Clara a sloppy kiss on the cheek.

"If Sammy had the hat on his head, how would Rosie get hold of it?" Mitch wondered.

Tom picked up the phone and called the station. Sammy the Grunt was somewhere in his neighborhood.

He requested police protection for the residence of Joe and Clara Skinner.

CHAPTER 47

HOME. LUCKY COULD feel it, he could smell it, and he could almost taste it. Just a little bit further, and he'd be with that special person who, in his dreams, kept calling him. Sensing her nearness was the fuel that was keeping him moving through the deep snow. When he did find her, he knew there would be food and a warm bed. As daylight faded into freezing black night, finding her was becoming more important

Tired, cold, and hungry, he plodded along, placing one foot ahead of the other, his stomach protesting its emptiness. Food. He needed food. When was the last time he'd eaten? He vaguely remembered the nice people who had been the last ones to feed him. Just thinking about the smell of food made his mouth water.

Lucky was a city dog; he knew that the things that whizzed by him on the road were things that would hurt him. Even though the snow was deeper in the ditch, that's where he walked.

Hearing a noisy thing approaching, he didn't even turn around to see what it was; he felt safe in the ditch.

IT WAS TOO warm in the cab of the snowplow. Mike Bell glanced at the clock on the dashboard; two more hours of plowing, and then he could go home. Would it ever quit snowing? The heat in the cab and the monotony of seeing nothing but white snow was hypnotic. When his eyes threatened to close, he jerked himself awake. He never should have stayed up last night watching a bad science-fiction movie. Yawning, he reached for the thermos of black coffee.

He never saw the dog that disappeared under the snow his plow had deposited in the ditch.

SNOW SLIDING OFF a branch landed on Sammy's face. With a startled cry, he sat up, sending several inches of wet snow flying. Where was he? Foggy memories weren't giving him many clues, but what he did know was that he'd never before been this cold. Sleeping in snow so full of water hadn't been the brightest thing he'd ever done. He could feel the icy condition of his wet clothes sticking to his body. Could he be this cold and live to tell about it?

His memory started to kick in when his effort to stand uncovered an empty beer bottle. How many of those bottles had he emptied? When another plop of snow fell off the tree and landed on his bare head, he reached up and touched it. A lump? Why did he have a good-sized lump on his head? A flash picture of himself landing on his butt after he'd smacked his head on an open cabinet drawer wasn't nearly as funny now as it had been when he was drunk. Was he sober now? He sure didn't feel tipsy; he just felt like he was coming down with something. The little nap that almost froze his ass had sobered him. All he had to show for his binge was a bad taste in his mouth.

His hand went back to his head. Hadn't he been wearing a woolen hat? Looking around, he didn't see it, and when digging through the new snow didn't produce it, he shrugged. Maybe he just dreamed that he'd worn one of the snitch's woolen hats. What he did uncover, though, was the snow bank where he had piled the contents from his pockets. The soggy book of matches reminded him of the one job he still had to do. Setting fire to the house, if he ever found the house, was going to be more difficult than he had figured in his drunken state.

His bladder had been full even before he had taken his nap. Sammy didn't even go behind the tree to relieve himself, but he did refrain from the juvenile urge to write his name in the snow.

He didn't have a watch, and with the sun hidden behind a black cloud, he had no idea how late in the day it was. He knew that he wasn't going to survive the freezing night in his wet clothes; he'd better find a vacant house…fast.

CHAPTER 48

CLARA HADN'T OPENED her eyes yet, but she was awake. Joe, sensing that she wasn't sleeping, tightened his arms around her and pulled her even closer. She had lost count of the times Joe had wakened her during the night to make love to her; her face felt raw from whisker burn.

"You awake?" he whispered.

"I'm afraid to say yes. Lord only knows what you'd do to me if I were awake," she teased.

"Clara, please don't ever leave me again. I can't tell you how much I missed you."

"I think you've made that pretty clear, love. But I wasn't gone *that* long."

He tightened his grip on her, "It sure seemed long to me!"

Silence.

"I'm sorry you didn't find your dog, hon."

"You do know that I had to try to find him, don't you?"

"I know. But sometimes I get jealous."

Silence.

"Clara, when you were growing up, did you ever have pets?"

Pets? She was puzzled. *After such a remarkable night, he wants to talk about pets?*

She turned her head to look at him. "Why the sudden interest in my past life?"

"Just humor me, Clara."

"Well, yes, I had pets. I had a cat, two canaries, one …."

"And what happened to them?" Joe asked quietly. He had a point to make, and he wanted to be as gentle as he could.

"What happened to them? Well, since pets don't live as long as humans do, they all died. The cat got sick, and I had to take her to the vet and have her put to sleep."

"That's a hard thing to have to do," Joe murmured.

"It was awful! I was holding her when the vet put the needle into her. She was so trusting! She was looking at me with such love, knowing that in all her life, I'd always looked after her…and here I was, ending her life. When her eyes closed and she was dead….well, I cried for days."

"How old was your cat?"

"I think she was over ten. We really didn't know, because she was a stray that just showed up one day and camped on our doorstep."

Silence.

"Do you have any idea how old Lucky is?"

"Well, I've had him for over five years, and he was a mature dog when he scratched on my office door."

"So, he could be around seven years old?" Joe figured.

"I would say so."

"Big dogs don't have as long a life span as small dogs. You do know that, don't you?"

Clara pulled herself out of Joe's arms and sat up. "What in the world are you getting at? Where is this conversation going?"

"Lucky is gone. If he never comes back, you will always remember him as he was when he disappeared."

"But he is coming back!" Clara cried. "Why is this nonsense coming out of your mouth?"

"Don't be so loud! We have lots of people in our house!"

"You can say that again! I'm tired of running a bed and breakfast! Why do they always end up in our house?"

"Shhhhhh."

"Really, Joe. What's your point?"

"Let's say Lucky does come back, and he lives to a ripe old age for what? Four more years? Five more years? And then, when he's old and sick, and you'd hung onto him for as long as you could, but eventually you'd have to do something to end his suffering, you'd end up at the vet's office, just as you did with your cat. Can you imagine holding Lucky in your arms and watching as life leaves his body?"

"Shut up, Joe! Just shut up!" Clara sobbed.

Joe grabbed her and held her close. "I'm just being realistic, Clara. Maybe if Lucky doesn't come back, you can always believe that he's alive and well, just living in someone else's home. That kind of an ending is a lot less painful than watching him die of old age."

She pulled away from him. "Take your hands off me! Don't touch me!" she shouted.

"Clara, calm down! You're thinking of Lucky as if he were human, but he's not, Clara, he's not a person, he's just a dog!"

Clara gasped.

Realizing what he just said, Joe's face turned white. Saying that Lucky was just a dog was an incendiary statement.

Clara got deadly still. "So Lucky is just a dog?" she asked in a quiet voice. "A dog that I should be glad is gone now so that I won't have to take care of him when he's old and sick? Did I get your message, Joe? Well, how about *this* message!"

Jabbing her finger into his chest, she raised her voice. "Why don't you leave while you're still relatively young so that I can always remember you this way? Then when you're an impotent, incontinent, and smelly old man, I won't have to take care of you. Now, did you get *my* message?"

Clara jumped out of bed before Joe could say anything in his own defense. He sat in bed, holding his head in his hands, while he listened to sobs coming from the locked bathroom.

THE EARLY RISERS were in the kitchen having their first cup of coffee, when loud voices from the bedroom directly above them caught their attention. It wasn't as if they were intentionally eavesdropping; the conversation was just so loud, it was impossible not to hear.

"Wow!" Mitch exclaimed. "Joe sure put his foot in his mouth with *that* statement!"

"How's he going to backtrack on that one?" Tom wondered. "Of all the things to say about Lucky! To Clara, that dog is anything but just a dog."

Marie spoke up. "But, guys, he *is* just a dog!"

Molly shrugged. "You'll never convince Clara about that. I've never seen anyone have as much love for an animal as she has for that dog. I'm not looking forward to having her sorry face back in the office, even though I'm swamped with having to work with all her buyers and sellers."

Tom's eyebrows were dancing up and down like red caterpillars. "Did anyone besides me have trouble sleeping last night?"

Marie frowned at her husband. "Tom, watch your mouth! After all, we're guests in their house."

Molly giggled. "Aw, come on, Marie! We all heard. I must say, Joe and Clara were pretty active last night."

A shout and the sound of something hitting the floor above their heads silenced the group around the table.

Marie made a face. "Sounds like a different kind of activity is going on up there now."

"Ouch," muttered Mitch.

One of the officers who'd spent the night on watch duty stuck his head into the room and interrupted the conversation.

Tom greeted his fellow officer. "Good morning, Don. Isn't your shift about over?"

"Good morning to you, too! Yes, my shift is over. But if anyone needs to go to their own house before going to work, I'd be happy to escort you."

Molly raised her hand. "I have a big buyer flying in from the west coast today. I need to grab an outfit out of my closet. Won't take but a minute."

"Can you be ready to leave in ten minutes?" Officer Jim asked.

"I'll be ready before then," Molly replied, "but I'll meet you there. I need my car for work today."

The rest of the breakfast crew ate in silence. How long was this insanity going to last? Not being allowed to enter their own house until Sammy was caught was getting old. Where was he?

CHAPTER 49

WHERE WAS SAMMY? It had been early evening when he'd finally stumbled upon a house that had no apparent activity going on inside. Knowing that if he intended to live until morning, he'd have to take a chance.

Getting into the house was easy. Once inside, he closed his eyes and smiled, waiting to feel the warmth that would melt his frozen body. When the warmth never materialized, his eyes flew open. It was just as cold in the house as it was outside! Looking around, he saw that sheets-covered objects were everywhere. A flip of a wall switch didn't produce light, and a turned facet didn't produce water. To top it all, the toilets bowls were filled with something that looked and smelled like a petroleum product. What kind of a house was this?

Sammy shivered and pulled his wet clothes close. This wasn't going to work. What he needed was a hot shower to thaw out his body, and a dryer to dry the snitch's wet clothes. From somewhere in his memory, the word "winterize'" swam to the surface, and he grabbed it. Yes, that was it. When a house wasn't going to be lived in during the winter season, utilities were stopped, the water was drained out of the pipes, and a solution was poured into the toilet bowls. All this was to prevent pipes from freezing and bursting. However, just remembering what the word meant didn't help him; he was still going to freeze to death.

Along with finding that there was no heat, no water, no food, or drink, he also found that there were no signs that a man lived in the house. He stood in front of a closet full of woman's lightweight summer clothes, and with no hesitation, he removed his wet ones. Could he be this cold and still live? With shaky hands, he grabbed things off their hangers and frantically dressed himself in layers of clothes so cold they felt almost wet against his skin.

By now, his whole body was shaking with violent shivers. Waves of exhaustion left him breathless, his legs didn't want to move, and he had an overpowering urge to sleep. It surprised him when he stumbled as he backed out of the closet. What was wrong with him? While trying to regain his balance, he backpedaled into a sheet-covered bed. Frantically, he tore off the sheet, hoping to find a blanket of some kind; there was nothing under the sheet but a bare mattress. There had to be blankets somewhere in the house!

What he did find on a shelf in one of the bedrooms was several lightweight quilts, and a sleeping bag. He used one of the quilts as padding on top of the cold mattress, wrapped the other quilt around him, and then tried to fit into the bag by pulling his long legs up to his chest. The interior of the bag was cold, but by now, Sammy's core temperature had dropped below what was required for normal metabolism, and sleep grabbed him.

A full bladder woke Sammy early the next morning. Alarmed when he opened his eyes and saw nothing, he thrashed around until he remembered he'd zipped the bag closed.

So, he'd survived the night. He was hungry and thirsty, he had no clothes except for what he had found in the lady's closet, and certainly no warm winter ones. The snitch's clothes were too wet to put on. A sneeze again reminded Sammy that the drunken nap in the snow had been really stupid.

The urge to urinate was too strong; no matter how much he hated to leave the warm bag, he had to go. Wrapping the quilt around him, he crawled out into the cold air and ran to the bathroom where he relieved himself on top of the petroleum solution in the toilet bowl, and then made a mad dash back for the bag.

His mad dash was cut short by the sound of a car's engine. The urge to return to the warmth of the bag was strong, but curiosity won. One look out the window…and his heart almost stopped: there was a police van in front of the house. How had they found him?

Should he stay where he was, or should he run? Stay? Run? The conflicting thoughts that were spinning through his head came to a screeching halt when a car pulled in front of the police van. Maybe they weren't coming for him after all?

Sammy took the time to run back and grab the other quilt, and then bundled up against the cold, he huddled by the window.

Wait! Didn't he know the lady who got out of the car and was walking through the deep snow on the unshoveled sidewalk with the cop. Yes! She was the redheaded sister of the snitch! What was her name? Molly! Yes, that was it, and she was the owner of that real estate office where the woman he used to call Miss Piggy worked. Miss Piggy was the owner of the huge dog. He hated that dog!

He had no idea why a policeman and Molly would be going into a house together… then it hit him. Cops buy houses, too, and didn't Molly sell houses for a living? Big deal. Here he'd gotten himself upset and excited, and all it turned out to be was a business transaction.

When his body began shaking with the shivers, he knew it was time to crawl back into the warm bag. He was about to turn away from the window, when he saw both the cop and Molly walking back to their vehicles. Molly was carrying something.

Sammy smiled while he watched the two cars drive away. He knew where there was a warm house just waiting for him.

It hadn't taken him long to find enough articles of clothing to keep him from freezing in the short run to the house next door. Getting in was a snap, and just walking into a warm house was such an emotional experience, tears were running down his cheeks.

The bathroom filled with steam as Sammy stood under the hot spray, warming his cold body. Finding clothes that fit was easy, and there were warm outer clothes to replace the snitch's wet ones. Thanking the man of the house for having good taste, he retreated to the kitchen. Ignoring several bottles of beer in the back of the refrigerator, he removed a container of leftover food, heated it up in the microwave, and settled in for a feast.

He was in the middle of drinking his second cup of freshly brewed coffee when he heard a car pulling into the driveway. The car door opened, and the redheaded woman climbed out. What was…Molly…yes, that's her name, up to? Why had she come back?

MOLLY, DRESSED IN the outfit that she'd retrieved from her closet, was speeding along toward the house she had scheduled to show to her big buyer. Oh, she wanted to make this sale! The house was the biggest and most expensive house in town, and just the thought of selling it made her heart race. All the details had been worked out; the buyer was going to meet her at the house, and she had already picked up the key….the key! Molly groaned, looked for a place in the road to turn around, and headed back toward her house. She had left the key at home. *Don't get rattled,* she told herself. *The key is not lost. I know where it is. I have lots of time to grab it, and still be on time for the showing.*

By the time Molly had unlocked the door and entered the house, Sammy had poured the almost full pot of coffee down the drain,

220

rinsed out his cup, and was hiding in the space under the desk in the room that obviously was an office.

Goosebumps appeared on his arms; this was just like playing hide-and-seek, his favorite childhood game. He heard the woman's footsteps as she passed the room where he was hiding…and then they stopped. Was she coming into this room? Yes, she was!

The sneeze that appeared out of nowhere startled Sammy, even though he was the one who had sneezed. He heard Molly stifle a scream.

Grabbing a heavy paperweight, he rounded the desk, and watched the surprised look on Molly's face dissolve into one of terror.

He looked down at the unconscious Molly on the floor, noted the blood puddle by her head, and figured that he had a few minutes to spend finding a phone book. From the map in the front of the book, he found Joe and Clara's house. It wasn't very far.

Twenty minutes later, Sammy, dressed in the man's winter clothes, was back outside in the cold. Should he take Molly's car and get out of town? It was tempting, but where would he go? Anything he did now only postponed the inevitable. Aware that with no money, and no friends, there was no chance of an ending with "and he lived happily ever after". No, after what he was about to do to the people who seemed to be living together in one house, he was finished. With a big resigned sigh, he accepted his fate.

According to the map, the house was just ahead. In a bag, he carried matches to start the fire, and a container of gasoline to help spread the fire. He wished he had a gun so that he could shoot anyone who tried to escape, but if the man of the house had a gun, Sammy hadn't found it.

———————

MIKE SHOOK HIS thermos and heard nothing. Coffee! He needed coffee! His blurry eyes tried to read the clock on the dashboard. Thirty minutes until the end of his shift was thirty minutes too many. One more sweep down this road was all he was going to do, and then back to the depot.

Despite himself, his eyes closed. He never saw the man who was looking over his shoulder, trying to get out of the way of the snowplow.

Sammy, running for his life, had a flash remembrance of Albert and Sarah scooping him up in their plow. He was yelling "Not again!" when the edge of the plow hit his head and deposited him, unconscious, in the ditch.

Mike jerked awake and pulled the truck back onto the road. Time to go to the depot.

CHAPTER 50

THE BREAKFAST CROWD hadn't yet left for work when the secretary at Allen Real Estate called. Molly's big buyer was wanting to know why Molly hadn't shown up for their appointment. Joe had answered the phone while he was still upstairs having a cold-shoulder-staring contest with Clara. The phone message had sent him yelling down the stairs, "Mitch, Molly never made it to her appointment!"

Mitch jumped up so fast his chair crashed to the floor. "Call 911! Have the police check on my house. In the meantime, I'm going home!"

"Not without me, you're not!" Tom yelled.

A police car pulled into the driveway as Mitch was backing out.

Mitch rolled down the car's window and yelled, "Get out of my way! This is an emergency!"

A uniformed officer crawled out of the car, and held up his hand. "Headquarters told me that I would probably find Mitch Hatch at this address. Are you Mitch Hatch?"

Mitch's face turned white. "She's dead, isn't she?" he whispered.

"No, Mr. Hatch, I just left your house. Your wife just has a huge bump on her head. She's on her way to the hospital."

Mitch covered his face with his hands. "Oh, thank God!" he sobbed.

Tom, who knew the officer, ran up to the car. "Hi, John! How did you know to go to Mitch's house?"

"A neighbor called. The whole town is edgy because they'd been warned. Since she didn't recognize the man she saw leaving Mitch's house, she called us."

Tom ran for his car.

"Might as well ride together," Mitch yelled to Tom. "Is Marie going?"

"No, she's staying back with the baby, and Joe went back upstairs, probably to continue the argument with Clara. Guess it's just the two of us."

CLARA JUMPED UP from her position on the floor when she heard Joe climbing the stairs. Curious about what was going on downstairs, she had stretched out with her ear on the register. Why hadn't Molly made it into work this morning? Had something happened at the real estate office? Whatever it was, she certainly wasn't going to ask shithead Joe about it.

She was off the floor and sitting on the bed by the time Joe walked into the room. Without looking at him, she remarked, "I see you're still around."

Joe heaved a huge sigh. "Of course I'm still around! Where would you want me to be, Clara?"

"Anywhere but here," she replied in a flat voice.

"I'm not going anywhere, so just let it go."

"Just let it go? I don't think so, Joe."

"I've apologized a dozen times. I truly am sorry for what I said, I shouldn't have said it, and I wish I could take it back, but I can't. What more do you want from me?"

"Just leave."

"You can't be serious!"

In a dead voice, Clara said, "Believe it."

"Well, now I know," Joe replied in a disgusted voice.

"Know what?"

"I always wondered if you loved your dog more than you loved me. Well, now I know."

Clara moaned; this was crazy talk. Of course she loved Joe! How could she confuse love for an animal with love for her mate? It was just that losing Lucky had made her insane with worry.

Turning, she held her arms out to him. "Joe...Joe...!" she implored.

He wasn't there. She heard the front door open and slam shut.

———————

CURLED UP WITH his tail over his nose trapping the heat against his body, Lucky had survived the night. He woke up to a cold, dark world. Was it a dream, or was he hearing familiar sounds? His survival instincts told him wherever he was, he needed to move. Since there was a layer of something over him, that wasn't easy. A wonderful smell hit his nose when Buddy poked his face into the hole he had scratched open in the deep snow. Once freed of the snow by two frantically digging pups, Lucky stood up and shook himself. He was freezing cold, his leg hurt, and he was weak from hunger, but he forgot it all for a moment while he greeted his pups. He could smell Lady on them; he needed to go home.

With the pups running ahead of him, he plodded along. They would only go so far before they'd run back and bark at him. He was so close to home, his heart was beating faster. Just a little bit further was the person who'd been calling him in his dreams; he could feel it.

But wait. What was that smell? It was a dark smell, a hated smell. It was coming from somewhere ahead of him in the ditch. He picked up the pace, his nose close to the snowy ground, and when he got to a certain spot, he began to dig; the two pups joined him.

———————

MOLLY WAS PROPPED up in bed, her red hair vivid against the white pillows. A bandage on her head was the only visible reminder of her run-in with evil.

Mitch stood in the doorway, just looking at his wife. Thinking about how close he had come to losing her brought tears to his eyes. He had waited a long time to find love, but love had come when he'd met Molly. At that time, Sammy the Grunt was trying to find Molly to kill her. He hadn't succeeded then, but he could have succeeded today.

Molly looked up and saw him watching her.

Holding out her arms, she waited; he just stood, staring at her.

"Come on, Mitch! I'm fine!"

Mitch rushed to her open arms and buried his face in her neck. Warm tears ran down her back.

"Mitch, really, I'm fine!"

"I'm angry with you! What happened to your police escort? Why were you in the house all by yourself?"

"Oh, Mitch, don't be angry with me, please! I had an appointment to show a house and I'd left the key at home. It never once entered my mind to call the police to go with me."

"I would have gone with you!"

"I know you would, but it didn't seem like such a big deal just to run in and get the key. I knew where I'd put it."

"I know, but if anything had happened to you…."

"Well, something did happen to me, but it was just a bump on the head."

"Do you remember anything?"

"I certainly remember the sneeze! It startled me, but before I could react, Sammy…." Molly cringed and touched her head. "Well, it happened so fast, that's all I remember. Does anyone know where he is?"

"No one has seen him since he left our house. That man has the ability to disappear; he just seems to vanish...until he pops up again."

"Wonder where he'll pop up next."

"Hopefully, when he does, someone will be around who can take him down...permanently."

———————

JOE MIGHT HAVE run out of the house, but he didn't run very far; no one had bothered to clear the sidewalk of snow. What a winter this has been! He couldn't remember another winter when there had been such a snowfall. Spring would bring some relief, but he could remember one late April when a blizzard had stopped everything. Michigan winters seem to go on and on and on and...wait a minute. Whose dogs were barking? He knew they couldn't be his dogs; he'd checked the dog addition and had seen Buddy and Rosie curled up with Lady. Really, people shouldn't allow their barking dogs to run loose. It was annoying, that's what it was.

He shivered. It was just too cold to stay outside. With thoughts of making up with Clara, Joe squared his shoulders and went back into the house

CHAPTER 51

LUCKY PACED AND sniffed, and sniffed and paced around what he and the pups had dug out of the snow. An offensive smell was motivating him to do something, but what? His nose was connecting the feelings of hate and pain. He couldn't remember what he had done, but whatever it was, it had made his special person very happy. She had given him praise, extra treats, and many pats on the head. He wanted to do it again.

The pups had no interest in the object they'd dug out of the snow. Home is where they wanted to go, but nipping at Lucky's hindquarters wasn't working.

Finally, one extra big sniff did it; Lucky remembered.

JOE STOOD OUTSIDE the bedroom door, trying to gather enough nerve to go inside and challenge Clara. There was no way in hell he was going to allow the Lucky issue to ruin the beautiful thing Clara and he had. He was well aware that making the statement that Lucky was "just a dog" was probably the biggest blunder of his life, but he had said it, and he couldn't take it back. If he had to apologize everyday for the rest of their lives, he'd do it.

Quietly, he opened the door and stepped into the room. Clara was lying across the bed, her face buried in her hands and her shoulders shaking with sobs. Stretching out beside her, he gently pulled her close.

"Oh, Joe! You came back!" she sobbed.

"You didn't really think I'd go, did you?"

"But, Joe, I said some terrible things to you...."

"Well, I said some pretty insensitive things, too."

"It's just...it's just that I'm half-crazy with worry. Can I plead temporary insanity?"

"You can plead anything you want, love, just as long as I know you love me at least as much as you love your dog."

Clara snickered. "It sounds funny when you say it like that. But, Joe, you have to know that the kind of love that I feel for Lucky is a different kind of love than I have for you."

Joe grinned and kissed her on the end of the nose. "Well, I can't tell you how relieved I am to hear that."

"Ah, come on, Joe. You knew that! But what you said about Lucky is true. If he never comes back, I will always remember him as he was the last time I saw him, and I'll try...I promise, I'll try...," she stopped to swallow a sob, "I promise I'll try to act more rational...and...and don't forget Buddy. Maybe he'll grow up to be just like his dad."

With love in his eyes, Joe whispered, "Can we kiss and make up now?"

The kiss was developing into the serious stage when the jarring of a ringing phone made Joe moan.

"Don't you dare answer it!" Clara whispered.

Joe didn't answer the phone, but Clarence did.

"Hey, someone on the phone wants to talk to either Clara or Joe," Clarence yelled outside their door.

"Tell them that we're busy!" Clara yelled back.

"They say it's important," Clarence insisted.

"Bummer."

"I'll take it," Clara said. "You just stay where you are, because I intend to come right back."

Listening to Clara's end of the conversation, Joe learned that someone was calling to complain about barking dogs, and it was the caller's opinion that the barking dogs belonged to them.

Clara hung up the phone and turned to Joe.

"Did you leave the pups out?"

"No, I didn't. I thought they were all asleep in the addition."

"Evidently, not so."

"Well, somebody must have...probably one of the vineyard people."

"You think we should go and see what they're up to?"

Joe sighed. "Wanna take a walk and cool off?"

Clara giggled. "It's below zero out there. How cold do you want to get?"

"Doesn't matter. I'll warm up fast when we get back."

Batting her eyelashes at him, Clara cooed, "Can I count on that?"

Bundled up against the cold, Clara and Joe headed in the direction of the barking pups. Since it was just one house away, they had no difficulty seeing Buddy and Rosie, barking at something in the ditch.

Joe commented as they trotted toward the noise, "I don't blame the neighbors for calling us. Wonder what has them so excited?"

As they approached, another bark, much deeper than that of the puppy's high-pitched sound, made Clara stop. Her eyes widened, her breath came in short gasps, and she fell to her knees.

Could it be? Could she believe her eyes?

There, sitting on top of something, was her dirty, mangy, and skinny dog.

THE WRATH OF WINTER

At the sight of his special person, his body wiggled, his tail wagged, and if a dog could smile, Lucky was smiling...but he stayed where he was.

"Joe! Oh, it's Lucky! It is! He's back! Oh, thank you, God!" Clara cried, rushing toward her dog.

Holding out his arm, Joe blocked her. "Hold on, Clara. That's a body he's sitting on. This could be a crime scene!"

Clara stopped short. "He's sitting on a body? Do you think that Lucky...."

"With that dog, who knows? Do you have your cell phone with you?"

Without taking her eyes off her dog, Clara handed a phone to Joe.

"Oh, Lucky! My dog! You're back!" she cooed. "You did come back to me!"

And then she asked the question that never, ever, would have an answer... "Where have you been all this time?"

Stepping a little closer, she looked at the bearded bald-headed man that Lucky was sitting on. Not recognizing him, she asked, "For God's sake, Lucky, what did you do this time?"

Joe bent down and studied the man's face. "Wanna bet that's Sammy the Grunt that your dog is sitting on?"

It was only after the police, the reporters, and the medical team had arrived on the scene that Lucky gave up his prime position on top of the frozen and dead body of Sammy the Grunt. Just as he'd remembered, he received a lot of praise. The special treats, the belly scratches, the pats on the head, and the love-hugs from his special person came later.

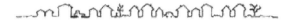

CHAPTER 52

CLARA WOKE WITH a start. Was he home? Was Lucky really home? As she jumped out of bed, she noticed that the other side was empty. Where was Joe? She'd figure that one out later, but right now, she had to see her dog.

The smell of wet dog hit Clara's nose as she stumbled into the dogs' area. Lucky was really there, but why was he wet? She kneeled in front of his sleeping form and held his huge head in her hands. Laying her forehead on top of his, she closed her eyes, breathed in the scent of her dog, and whispered a thankful prayer. Lady woke up, sniffed, and went back to sleep; Lucky didn't stir.

Looking for a cup of coffee and breakfast, Clara entered the kitchen and found Joe already there.

"Morning, Joe! I was surprised to find your side of the bed empty this morning. Were you called into work?"

Joe was leaning against the kitchen counter, the newspaper spread out in front of him. "No, a call from the station didn't get me out of bed, but the smell of a dirty dog did."

Clara scrunched up her nose. "He *was* smelling a bit gamy. But let me guess. You took Lucky to the station and the guys gave him a bath. Right?"

"You guessed it! Hey, come and look at the pictures of your dogs. Buddy and Rosie got into the action, too."

"Front page again?"

"As always! I swear, Lucky looks as if he's smiling."

In Clara's eagerness to see the picture, she bumped Joe's hand. The coffee that splashed out of his cup landed on an article below the fold in the paper. They probably wouldn't have noticed it anyway, because it was about Mike Bell, a man they didn't know, receiving an award for his five accident-free years of plowing the town's roads.

"Sorry about that!" Clara apologized and grabbed a paper towel. "Does it say why Sammy was in the ditch?"

"The officials are calling it a hit-and- run accident. Seems he had some kind of head injury."

"Was it the head injury that did him in?"

"Indirectly it did. If it had been a warm summer night, Sammy would have had a bad headache when he woke up. But unfortunately for him, it wasn't a warm summer night."

"And Lucky, coming from only God knows where, stumbled onto his frozen body?"

Joe shrugged. "Since neither Lucky nor Sammy is talking, that's the story."

Clara grinned as she studied the pictures. "That's my dog! God, I'm glad he's home!"

Joe hugged her. "Are you going into work today?"

"I have to. Reporters from all over are coming to interview me. So Lucky has to go with me."

"I hope he stays awake while all this is going on. I had a hard time waking him this morning to take him for a bath."

"I just checked on him. He's one tired dog!"

Later that day, when Clara was being interviewed at work, she once again stood in front of the Allen Real Estate sign. Lucky was the talk of the town, and the phones at the office were ringing off their hooks. Molly's mother, Peggy, was back at work answering the phones, and Mitch's mother, Marilyn, was in the back room of the office doing her magic on the computer.

Marilyn called out to Peggy at the front desk, "Just like old times! Isn't this fun?"

"It sure is!"

Silence.

"Marilyn, what are we going to do when Lucky gets too old to do wild things that bring in business and gives us jobs?"

"Hmmm. Well, there's Buddy...."

Clara rolled her chair to the open doorway of her office and asked the two women, "What's this I hear about Lucky getting old?"

Peggy shrugged. "Well, aren't we all? I was just bemoaning the fact that eventually Lucky will get too old to go off on adventures. By the way, have you made any headway in finding out how he got to Ohio?"

"Not a clue. And how did he get back? I was in Rochester Hills the same time he was, and he made it home as fast as I did. How? "

"And I suppose he's not talking," giggled Marilyn.

The door flew open, and Molly breezed in, waving a legal-sized paper.

"I did it!" she crowed. "I just sold the most expensive house in our little town! My west coast buyer didn't even counter the asking price! Can you beat that?"

"Wow!" Clara's eyes were big. "You commission check is going to be a beauty!"

Marilyn cleared her throat. "It's probably none of my business, but since I am your mother-in-law and thus a part of your family, may I ask what you're going to do with all that money? Pay down the mortgage on your house?"

Molly laughed. "No, that would be much too sensible. So, Grandma Marilyn, this is what I'm thinking. Just your son, his two nieces, and I will go to Disney World."

"Oh, how wonderful!" Marilyn cried. "But wait a minute! You didn't mention the twins. What about them?"

Molly smiled sweetly at her mother-in-law. "I was thinking we'd just leave the twins at home with you."

Marilyn jumped up so fast her chair hit the floor. "Oh, no you don't!" she yelled.

The office rang with laughter. "Thank you, Grandma Marilyn, for the good laugh," Molly said while wiping her eyes. "You can relax; we aren't going to Disney World. I probably *will* use the commission money to pay down the mortgage, but you were fun to watch."

"Harrumph!" muttered Marilyn as she turned back to her computer.

Clara rolled her chair back to the doorway. "Anyone hear from Tom and Marie?"

Peggy was on the phone, so Marilyn answered. "Yes, I did! They're living in a motel until their house is cleaned up. Their homeowners' insurance policy is covering everything, even the motel bill."

Peggy hung up the phone. "That was Sarah that I was talking to. She said she was so used to being around people, it felt strange to be once again isolated out there on the vineyard. She said to say 'hi' to all of you."

"That's it? Nothing else?" asked Clara.

"What did you want her to say?"

"Something about a puppy."

"Why should she be talking about a puppy?"

Clara shook her head. "I hope they make good on their promise to Clarence. If anyone can understand how much a person can love a dog, it's me." She chose to ignore several pairs of rolling eyes. "When the vineyard people were leaving my house to go back home, they couldn't find Clarence...and then I realized Buddy wasn't around, either."

"Let me guess," Peggy interrupted. "Clarence didn't want to be separated from the pup."

"It was a sad scene, believe me. That's when Sarah and Albert promised Clarence he could have a dog. I hope they keep their promise."

Peggy grinned. "Would it make you feel better if I told you that there was a lot of background noise while I was talking to Sarah?"

"I guess it depends on the noise. What was it?"

"A barking puppy!"

From his big bed in the corner of her office, Lucky was watching his special person. Oh, how he'd missed her! Inside of him was a feeling of comfort that had absent while he was away. But lying here, he could feel it growing inside him, along with the sense that all was well. Where he was right now was where he was supposed to be.

But the best part? The best part was that, once again, he had done something that had made his special person happy...very happy.

CPSIA information can be obtained at www.ICGtesting.com
Printed in the USA
BVOW070916241212

309012BV00001B/3/P